# DOUBLE D SHOWDOWN

Zach sensed there was bad trouble. Just how bad he began to find out when he drove his buggy into the run-down town and ran foul of Bronco Parks, foreman of the Double D. Small-time ranchers and sodbusters were moving out — Dan Dawson, the new owner of the Double D ranch, was making offers that few could refuse if they wanted to stay alive. The sheriff had been murdered and nobody wanted to be the lawman — until Zach made it his task to right the wrongs.

# Books by Ed Hunter
## in the Linford Western Library:

## BULLION MASSACRE

ED HUNTER

# DOUBLE D SHOWDOWN

## Complete and Unabridged

LINFORD
*Leicester*

First published in Great Britain in 1993 by
Robert Hale Limited
London

First Linford Edition
published November 1995
by arrangement with
Robert Hale Limited
London

British Library CIP Data

Hunter, Ed
Double D showdown.—Large print ed.—
Linford western library
I. Title II. Series
823.914 [F]

ISBN 0-7089-7764-2

Published by
F. A. Thorpe (Publishing) Ltd.
Anstey, Leicestershire

Set by Words & Graphics Ltd.
Anstey, Leicestershire
Printed and bound in Great Britain by
T. J. Press (Padstow) Ltd., Padstow, Cornwall

This book is printed on acid-free paper

To my pal Peter Daly
Thanks for always believing in me.

To my pal Peter Daly
Thanks for always believing in me

# 1

IT was not usual for Bronco Parks, hard-case foreman of the Double D ranch, to be riding into town during the heat of the early afternoon. It was still less usual for him to be bringing in a mean-looking bunch of cowhands during working hours. Anyone with half an eye could tell they had nothing in mind except trouble.

Worried townsfolk, conscious of potential danger, didn't know what kind of trouble. But to normal, peace-loving folks, trouble was trouble, in any guise. Like dust driven by the wind, the locals drifted off the street. Then they stood watching safely from sheltered positions on the shaded boardwalks, or partly concealed in doorways as the mounted mob moved relentlessly on, along Main Street.

"There's his wagon," one of the

1

riders called out, pointing to a farm wagon standing by the side of the road up ahead.

"Yeah, that's his rig, all right," Bronco agreed. "We'll wait there for 'im." Laughing and joking, they swung down from their saddles then went around to the other side of the hitching rail and rolled untidy cigarettes while they told bunk-house jokes.

Suddenly the bell on the door of the only mercantile left in the town, jangled. When the waiting men looked they saw a figure they recognized hold the door open with his foot as he backed out on to the boardwalk. He was laughing and carried a sack of flour on his shoulder.

"See ya next month, Harry," he called into the store. "Be back then for that new plough." The door swung shut and he turned, blinking in the sun, to look towards his wagon. His laughter died as he saw the Double D hands. Below the broad twisted brim of his weekday hat, his face clouded over as it set in a scowl. "Scum," he muttered, then with his eyes focused straight ahead, made resolutely for his wagon.

"Well, will y'all look here fellas," Bronco sneered. Pushing his hat to the back of his head, he spoke to the farmer. "See you've been buyin' a whole heap of stuff." Then he grinned, displaying twisted and chipped teeth, stained brown from years of chewing tobacco. "You rich or somethin', Naylor? Or you started wisin' up, and buyin' enough supplies to get you an' your kinsfolk back east again where ya came from?" He pushed himself upright, grinned at his men, then stepped arrogantly out directly into the nester's path. Slouching, hands on hips, he spat a stream of tobacco juice towards the oncoming man's feet, narrowly missing them.

As though given a secret signal, the others moved from the rail. Flexing their fingers and ominously rubbing

3

at their knuckles, they clenched their fists in readiness as they circled both the nester and the foreman, closing in to form a human fence.

"Out of my way, boy." The homesteader was lean and as tough as whipcord, but the white hair which showed from under his hat told that he was no longer a young man, nor was he as big or as powerful as the one who opposed him. But neither was he a coward. With his free hand he pushed his aggressor to one side and marched on.

He had only taken a couple of steps when Bronco made a grab for the sack of flour, then pulled hard enough to spin him around and overbalance his load. As the sack fell to the ground the ranchhands laughed and jeered. Then grimly, like a bunch of hungry coyotes moving in on a wounded jack-rabbit, they all began to punch and jostle him around the ring. One snatched the farmer's hat and called out an invitation to the others.

"Hey, guys. Go for it." With that he threw the hat spinning high into the air and drew his gun. Others followed suit and there were wild yells and whoops of delight as the hat jerked about in its flight. Pinpoints of daylight could be seen through the crown and brim as it was riddled with lead. Loud-mouthed boasting accompanied raucous laughter, and the air around them hung heavy with the acrid stench of powder smoke.

★ ★ ★

Zach heard the gunfire shortly before he drove his buggy around the corner on to Main Street. Things don't change much, he thought, remembering the last time he had passed this way. That had been five years before, when he and Lo Ming, his Chinese cook, had been huntin' the Masterson gang. He could not suppress a grin as he recalled the little man. Then the grin disappeared as he looked ahead at the

5

gang roughing up a man of middle height.

The rowdies were too intent on their fun to notice the buggy as it drew up behind them. Two of them held the badly beaten homesteader by his arm, with his back pressed against the hitching rail, while the others watched their ranch foreman.

"Hold 'im good, boys," Bronco grinned. "We's gonna see how this nester mixes us a fancy cake." With that he raised his foot above the fallen flour sack, then plunged the spiked rowel of his Mexican spur into it. "We'll just get the ingredients ready first." With a sneer of evil intent, he dragged his heel viciously back. The spur split the sack completely along its length, and finely-ground flour trickled out to spill on to the earth.

Bronco's foot had hardly lifted clear of the sack when a rifle shot cracked out, from outside the group, but nearby. The bullet tore the heel from under his fancy hand-tooled boot, on the foot he balanced on. The next thing he knew, he was on his back, rolling among the dust and horse manure which coated the dirt road.

The laughing stopped. Everyone gawped and twisted around to see Zach standing up on his buggy. A smoking Winchester was in his hands and it still pointed their way.

"Get 'em up fellas," he suggested laconically, then still keeping a keen watch on them, he stepped down, left the carbine behind on the driving seat and drew the .45 Colt from his right-hand holster. With this formidable weapon securely gripped in his fist, he moved in silently among them, covering them, his eyes daring any one of them to make the slightest move.

Bronco cursed. For one tense moment it looked as though he would be brave enough to make a try as he slid his right hand part way towards his own gun.

"Try," coaxed Zach. " . . . an' you're dead."

The ranch foreman opened both

hands. He grimaced and shrugged, then slowly raised them, to just below shoulder height.

"Hold it, fella. We ain't got no score t' settle with you." Sitting up slowly, he licked his lips while his eyes still fixed on the unwavering gun barrel. "We ain't harmin' you," he argued. "You ain't got no right t' buy in to this deal."

"By my way o' counting, I'd say you've got the deck in this game a mite too loaded in your favour," Zach reasoned. "All of ya, ranged up on one unarmed man." He pointed at the two holding the injured homesteader. "You two. Let him be."

"Don't know who y'are mister," the released man said out of the corner of his bruised and bleeding mouth, after he had crossed to stand alongside Zach, "but I'm sure glad you bought in when ya did."

"Know how to use one of these?" Zach asked, offering the gun from his left-hand holster. "Reckon you could

8

hit anyone from here?"

"Friend," the injured man said loud enough for all to hear, then he winked, "At this range I can shoot the little toe off a mosquito's middle left foot."

"You. Up on your feet," Zach ordered. Seeing Bronco obey, he waved him across to the horse trough beside the hitching rail. "Get in."

"Not on your life," the ringleader snarled.

Bang! The other boot lost its heel and once more its owner grovelled in the horse dung.

"In, I said." The silence was threatening. The hammer of the Colt clicking to full cock was heard by everyone around. "In . . . if you don't want to be dancin' about with a toe missin'."

"I'll remember you mister," Bronco warned, as with a glare of hate he climbed, to stand up to his knees in the water-filled trough. Bystanders who had gathered on the boardwalk began to laugh outright. At this, he screamed

9

with rage. "You better believe me, I'll fix you good mister."

Zach was neither worried nor impressed. He nodded down at the murky water in the trough and spoke quietly.

"Lay down an' shut your fool mouth."

"I ain't gonna!"

"Believe me, you is!" The pistol barrel swung in line with Bronco's kneecap and the finger began to curl and tighten around the trigger.

"All right, all right," Bronco growled through clenched teeth as reason overcame his pride. "Hold it!" Throwing his reputation to the wind, he splashed down angrily into the water. At the same time, he was aware of the many shaming jeers and loud laughter of the townsfolk. To add to his chagrin, his own men were cheering too.

"Out!" Zach jerked the gun barrel upwards.

Drenched, with his hair flattened down over his eyes and his feet squelching inside his boots, Bronco clambered out. With his eyes blazing with hate, he stood with the water pooling around him, turning the dust to mud.

The pistol barrel was jerked again. This time it was pointed down and aimed at the split flour sack.

"You owe this fella," the buggy man spoke out. Catching sight of the white-aproned storekeeper close by, he added, "Now I think a generous fella like you, will be glad t' pay what's due and buy a new poke of flour."

"Oh no!" Bronco stepped back, more water squelching noisily from his boots.

"Oh yes!" Zach persisted.

"Not on your life. I ain't feedin' no nester's brood."

The Colt barked once, spitting out a bullet which grooved the extreme front edge of the soaked man's left boot sole, then buried itself in the dirt. There was no more argument. Bronco, white-faced and hanging on to his self-control by the thinnest of threads, looked over to the store keeper.

"Put that flour on my tab, Harry."

Harry nodded gravely, then hurried back inside the mercantile as the crowd of watchers, sensing the excitement was all over, began to disperse.

"Now hit the trail before someone gets hurt around here," Zach advised them. "And don't get any fancy notions about using your guns. I'll be watchin' you all the way."

Without further opposition the mob mounted up and high-tailed it out of town without a backward glance.

"Reckon them fellas are glad to get away from you mister." The smiling homesteader returned the pistol, butt first, and uncocked. Then he offered his hand. "Naylor's the name . . . Josh Naylor. I'm mighty beholdin' to ya for helpin' out like ya did."

"Friends call me Zach." He slid the twin Colts into their holsters then shook the outstretched hand firmly.

"Zach?" The nester's eyebrows shot up. His mouth gaped and he looked around at the buggy. "Hell's fire, I should've knowed it."

"You've heard of me?" There was surprise in Zach's voice.

"Sure. You're the buggy man! That Chinese neighbour o'mine, he's been tellin' me all about ya. What you both did to that Masterson gang." He suddenly looked serious again. "You come t' help us, just like he said ya would?"

★ ★ ★

Ten miles out, on the other side of town, they turned off the stage road. They entered a well-grassed valley, down the centre of which, an idyllic clear-water creek sparkled and splashed over the rocks breaking its surface.

"Best dang parcel of land in the territory," Josh Naylor said proudly. "An' I own all this side of the creek right up to them hills yonder. Your pal the Chinaman, he holds title to the other side, across the water."

13

Memories stirred in Zach's mind as he recalled the spread he had once owned and the effort he had put into it. That had been before Greg Masterson's renegades had ended it all. He had hunted them down and had taken his revenge, but revenge hadn't replaced his murdered wife and unborn child. Nor had it given him enough peace of mind to let him settle down to build another ranch.

It wasn't the money which held him back. There was plenty of cash just lying idle in two or three banks, but money didn't interest him. He was no coward yet was afraid to latch on to another woman and start a new life, in case it all happened once more. It would be a long time before he'd ever really settle again . . . if he ever did.

"Yes, sir, been a sodbuster all my life," Josh crowed as he drove his unsprung farm cart alongside the elegant and smooth-running buggy. "Never knowed anythin' else, an' never wanted anythin' else." Then

14

his tone altered as he grew angry and continued, "Until Dan Dawson, God rot his hide, blowed in an' won the Double D ranch in a poker game."

"What happened t' the fella who lost the place?" Zach wanted to know.

"Some reckon he blew his brains out in the livery behind the saloon that same night, because he couldn't face tellin' his wife," the nester explained. "I can't stomach that notion. It don't seem to sit right somehow. He wasn't like that."

"You think he was murdered?"

"Sure do. But there ain't nothin' I can do about it, is there? I ain't got no silver star pinned on my vest."

"Well, where's the sheriff?" Zach asked. "I noticed he didn't show up when them fellas were shootin' their guns off back there."

"He would've scared the shit out of 'em if he had," the farmer said his face remaining deadpan. "He's been buried on Boot Hill for close on a year." Philosophically he hunched his

15

shoulders in an expressive shrug. "The sheriff was another obstacle to Dan Dawson. Everybody knew that, so we weren't surprised when he ended up dead in an alley one night with a bullet hole through his badge."

"And no one," Zach reasoned, "would take on the badge after that?"

"Dead right," Josh Naylor answered. "Not at any price. They say the mayor practically begged the deputies one at a time, to take the top star. But they wouldn't have it. Every one of 'em quit. Since then only the town drunk ever uses the sheriff's office . . . to sleep off a hangover. After that, it was all downhill and an open town as far as the Double D was concerned."

For a time Zach drove his buggy in silence. Then he looked across at his companion.

"What happened next, after Dawson moved in?"

"What you'd expect with a snake like that?" Josh said bitterly. "Next morning, just after sun-up, Dawson

16

rides in with his mob, sacks all the ranchhands and puts the widder woman and her clothes on a broken-down old wagon, an' sends her off the place. God knows where."

He shook his reins, flapping them sharply on the broad backs of his team, speeding them up to keep abreast of the buggy. "And since then, every mortal thing's changed around here. People went missin'. Decent, well-established folks, some wi' young families, have been forced to sell out to him for less than the price of scrub land." He jerked his thumb back over his shoulder. "Did ya not notice how many places were boarded up when we came on through the town?"

"Yeah, sure did. The place's lookin' a mite sad an' run down since last I rode out this way." Zach remembered how lively and prosperous it had once been. "I guess if there ain't s'many folks around, the business side of things in town's bound to fold first and move on out."

A rider suddenly came into view over a rise in the ground ahead. He was standing in the stirrups, riding hard, waving and coming straight towards them.

"Pa!" the rider yelled loudly and clearly while still some considerable distance off and Zach knew it wasn't a man at all. The voice belonged to a young woman and from the strident note of it, a distressed one. "Pa, we got more trouble. Riders from the Double D, they've been an' flattened our crops."

"G'damn!" Josh Naylor swore as his daughter expertly reined in hard, just in time to prevent colliding with his rig. But he kept the wagon moving without checking its speed. "Anyone hurt?"

"No Pa, just the crops," she panted. "No warnin' or nothin'. You'll see for yourself. They just drove them steers straight through the fields like they wasn't there, then away again."

"Were ya there? Did you see 'em do it?" the dirt farmer asked.

"No. Didn't have to," she was quick to retort. "Like I told ya, it's a mess. The corn an' the tobacca . . . everythin's just been stomped into the ground."

"Could've been an accident," Zach offered as an explanation. "Maybe the herd went there on their ownsome. It happens from time t' time."

"Mister," she called from the other side of the wagon, twisting her mouth with more than a little disdain, "it might have escaped your notice, but I'm a fully-growed woman. I know the difference between cattle and horse sign, and some of them hoof prints showed iron shoes . . . horseshoes!" As if to show her contempt for his male attitude, she pressed her point home. "Another thing! I ain't ever come across no steer that bothered to stop an' lift out fence posts, to make a gateway."

"Here, gal, watch your mouth. You be more respectful when you're a-talkin' to your elders," Josh admonished his forthright daughter. "This here's Lo Ming's friend, the fella he's always spoutin' off about."

"The buggy man?" Her face lit up as she smiled. "Hey, you're not expected for another couple o' days at least." On impulse she rode around and offered her hand, positive, like a man would. "Hi. I'm Ellie."

The buggy man tipped his hat and smiled. He reached out then shook her hand.

"And I'm Zach, ma'am," he told her. "Glad to know ya."

Ellie glanced across at her father and a sudden look of concern came to her face.

"Pa, I never noticed till now: you've been hurt. What's happened?"

"Nothin' much, but it could've been," he informed her. "Bronco Parks and some of the fellas from the Double D were hazin' me." He nodded to indicate Zach. "Must've been my lucky day. This fella, he appeared out of the blue and bought in without bein'

20

asked . . . sent 'em all packin' with their tails between their legs." He laughed as he went on, "Made Bronco take a bath in a horse trough. And on top o' that, forced 'im to pay for a sack of flour he spoiled."

"He did?" Ellie, elated, turned her attention back to Zach again. She didn't beat around the bush. "Mister I could kiss ya."

By this time they had topped the rise where Ellie had first come into view. Now, as though planned to relieve Zach's embarrassment, the diminutive figure of his Chinese friend could be seen on the other side of the creek. He was driving a small herd of good-looking brood mares along the bank.

From the top of the rise they watched as Lo Ming reined in his horse. Shielding his eyes with his hand he gazed up at them as if in disbelief. For a couple of seconds he sat in the saddle, still as a statue. Then recognition dawned. Deserting the mares, he charged like a madman into the shallow waters of the creek. Splashing across, he sent rock and water flying, soaking himself and his horse in his frantic urge to greet his friend.

"Hi, Boss." He grinned broadly, panting after his mount had thundered up the steep slope then pulled alongside the elegant buggy.

"Hi, pal. It's been a long time." Zach's answer was gruff and spoken with genuine feeling. They shook hands warmly, and he added, "I hardly knowed ya, all dressed up like a regular bronco-buster. You're turnin' into a real Yankee-doodle American." Before he could say anything more, the delighted Chinaman twisted around in his saddle to beam at the dirt-farmer and his daughter.

"You see," he exclaimed proudly, "When Lo Ming say Boss come to help. He tell truth." With a theatrical wave of his arm he pointed to the buggy. "I not lie. Boss here plenty quick in fine buggy . . . Fix Double D gang, damn good."

# 2

THE riders of the Double D kicked their heels in the dust and waited outside the ranch-house as they listened to the tirade of colourful invective which kept gusting to them from inside.

"The boss's givin' Bronco a real roastin' since he got back from Santa Fe this mornin'," Bartlet, one of the younger men, sniggered to Kansas Smith, his buddy. "Seems he thinks Bronco can't cut the mustard any more."

Kansas Smith sniffed hard, and wiped the back of his hand on a developing dewdrop which had quivered for some time on the end of his turned-up nose. He sniffed again then had to spit before giving his judgement.

"Yeah, maybe there'll be a good job goin' for the askin' shortly, eh?" He nudged a wizened oldtimer who sat on the side of the half-empty horse trough, patiently whittling away at a stick with an ancient skinning knife. "You thinkin' o' takin' over the job as top hand, Abe?"

Old Abe cocked his head to one side, pushed his hat brim back, closed one eye, then peered up at the kid.

"Kansas, if I was you boy," he began, his tone threatening, "I'd be careful 'bout what ya let out of that big mouth of yours." He started to cut at the piece of wood again. "If Bronco was t' hear you, or somebody t' mention it to 'im, you'd pull line duties on ya lonesome for six months straight . . . after you'd lost some teeth."

"Huh," the kid smirked arrogantly, but it was all show. "You don't scare me none, Gran'pa, an' neither does he." Kansas jabbed his thumb at his own chest, sneered and announced for all to hear, "Nobody makes me eat crow."

Abe laughed, and was about to make

24

a stinging remark to put the youth in his place. But before he could, the ranch-house door opened and the foreman stormed out, clenching and unclenching his fists in frustration, his face and neck more red than usual.

"Mount up," Bronco barked as he pulled on his riding gloves, "an' y'all better be loaded for bear." He stopped his harangue for a moment, looked around at them and suddenly pointed at Kansas Smith. "You," he snapped, "go saddle my horse, and get the lead out of your arse, we ain't got all day."

"Yes sir. Right away," the youth answered without a hint of rebellion. He skittered like a scalded cat to where the foreman's saddle rested on the top rail of the corral.

In no time at all he returned at the run, leading the horse at the trot all saddled and ready. Kansas steamed past the oldtimer who laughed outright. Already mounted, waiting with the others, Abe remarked, "For a sassy young fella, who don't chew on crow shit from no one ... ya sure as hell seem t' have a mighty hearty appetite."

* * *

Josh Naylor had worked steadily beside the fields of trampled crops since shortly after sunrise. Without stopping for rest he drove himself on, digging holes, and driving in fence posts. At each section he strung fresh barbed wire, then, ratcheting the lever of his Sylvester, stretched each strand until it sang to his touch like a tuned string on a guitar.

The last staple was being hammered into a section of fence when the nester's work was interrupted.

"Made a real good job of that, didn't ya Pop?" Bronco sneered from close behind. "But you know Mr Dawson don't like barbed wire on his land."

"This is my land," Josh Naylor told him.

"Your land?" Bronco Parks did his usual spit. "You don't own nothin'. You're a nester. Nesters don't own, they just steal good range land with government help." He started to dismount.

Josh's fist choked the handle of his hammer as he stepped towards the ranch foreman.

"Yeah, the US Government," the settler declared for all to hear. "And they say I please myself what I do on it . . . or who comes on it." He raised the hammer as a warning. "So go on, get movin' and leave the way ya come."

A ripple of sound passed along the men facing him, as like a well-rehearsed drill, they slapped leather, drew their guns and pointed them directly at Josh. He stopped walking and let the hammer lower to his side. It had been a useless gesture and he knew it.

"Drop it," Bronco ordered, as he stood by his horse. "Drop it, before my boys here blow your danged fool head off'n them shoulders." With the

27

supreme arrogance of the bully, he strolled over until he was close enough to dig his pistol in the farmer's belly. "Drop it."

The pistol dug savagely hard and Josh could not help but grunt at the sudden pain. The hammer slipped from his grip and dropped to the ground with a thud. In a haze of anger he could only stand and endure the verbal torments. To do anything else would, he knew, invite immediate death from a hail of bullets. Head up, he gritted his teeth and stared back into Bronco's flint-like eyes.

"Big man, ain't ya, Bronco?" the nester gasped, still defiant. "But then your sort always is against an unarmed man, with a gun in your hand and a pack o' no-good coyotes backin' your play."

"An' you, ya think you're Jesus Christ." Without any warning, striking with whiplash speed, the foreman of the Double D smashed the side of his revolver barrel alongside the nester's head. There was an instant show of blood. The defenceless homesteader's eyes glazed. He seemed to fold. Then slowly he sagged down on to his knees before pitching forward on to his face in the dusty, sun-warmed earth.

Slickly, full of confidence in himself, Bronco holstered his weapon. With a grin he twisted around to face the others.

"Well, y'all know how much the boss hates barbed wire. What you waitin' for? Got it taken down." He pointed at a Mexican and young Kansas, then motioned them to him with a crooked forefinger. "Manuel, you remember that other dirt-farmer who was givin' us all that sass, the one over at Indian Falls?" he prodded the Mexican.

"*Si, señor.*" Manuel's sadistic smile split his swarthy, pock-marked features to display two gold teeth. His normally sombre black eyes widened. They looked wild, and glowed from the memory. "*Si*, I remember muy *bien*."

"I want this dirt-scratcher" — the foreman pointed the toe of his high-heeled boot at his recumbent and bloody victim — " . . . dealt with exactly like that." looking around at the cultivated land, he went on, "Once homesteaders get their greedy claws into a piece o' range land, they don't leave no room for cattle. An' we's cattle men." He spat again. "His kind, hell . . . they're like mules, but inclined to be more than a mite stubborn." He kicked Josh in the ribs. "Yessir. I've a mighty powerful feelin' this one's a real mule head. He's gonna need a whole heap lot of persuadin'."

\* \* \*

Zach suffered as he was given the grand tour of Lo Ming's horse ranch by its proud owner. Unlike when driving his well-sprung and comfortable buggy, riding horseback he was never really able to relax. The old bullet wounds, particularly those in his legs, although healed long ago, still pained him from time to time, especially when he sat a saddle. Once again he silently cursed the man who had shot the four bullet holes into him: Captain Greg Masterson.

Twisting a little in his saddle, Zach eyed Lo Ming as the Chinaman chatted non-stop, pointing out the improvements he had carried out, and other future plans for the ranch. Masterson was dead, killed long ago by the little Chinese wrangler who now rode at his side. Lo Ming had saved his life that night in the mountains by blasting the southern renegade captain at the last moment with his twelve-gauge. Although glad to be alive, on the other hand, Zach secretly harboured some resentment. He had never quite been able to forgive his friend for killing the man and robbing him of his revenge.

"Boss. Boss?"

Ming's concerned voice broke into

31

Zach's thoughts. He blinked and struggled to think of where he was, and what he was doing.

"Yeah," Zach answered with a start, "what's on your mind?"

"Smoke. You smell it?" the Chinaman asked, frowning. "You not smell?" he persisted in a puzzled voice.

The skin on the bridge of Zach's nose wrinkled as he sniffed the air. After the third attempt he nodded.

"Sure. It's wood smoke."

A gunshot cracked out, shattering the silence. It came from about half a mile away, carried on the wind from the same direction as the smell. Before the echo had died away into the distance along the valley, another shot rang out, apparently from the same gun.

Open-handed, Lo Ming made a chopping motion with his arm to point over at his neighbour's land. Between them and whoever had fired the gun, the land undulated on the other side of the creek.

"Come on." Forgetting the stabbing twinges of pain, Zach kicked his horse into a sharp gallop. "That don't sound like good news t' me." Right behind him, Lo Ming kept pace, as together they raced towards the creek. At the point where they entered, the water was close to shoulder-deep and the unwilling horses struggled. The riders pressed them on, ignoring the discomfort to either themselves or the animals. Both men knew Josh Naylor was not the type to ever carry a gun, so any shot fired was a sure bet to spell out trouble.

Noisily the horses emerged from the shallows at the other side, their hooves clattering on the rocks while water splashed in every direction. The riders urged the horses up the rise as though their lives depended upon it. As they travelled, both men unshipped their carbines from the saddle holsters and levered shells into the chambers, ready.

Shortly they found themselves riding into thin clouds of drifting wood smoke.

Their blowing mounts attempted to veer away from the fumes, but were held to their course.

When they had crested the last ground ripple, Zach pulled up and scanned the scene before him.

"Jesus," he breathed out in disgust.

There was no sign of any gunman, but up ahead of them, a bonfire of all but two of the newly-cut fence posts blazed away. One post remained standing in the earth as Josh had originally driven it. The second was fixed at right angles to the first, close to the top, forming a cross. Secured to this cross, could be seen a human form.

"It's Josh," Lo Ming confirmed as they rode at an extended gallop to the nester's aid.

★ ★ ★

The only parts of his body that Josh Naylor was able to move were his lips and eyes, and even the use of these

34

was limited. His whole body had been secured to the fence post by lengths of twisted barbed wire, stapled every few inches along the wood. After this had been done, the Mexican and his young helper had wrapped coil after coil of the viciously spiked wire, binding their helpless prisoner in great cocoons from which it would be impossible for him to escape on his own. Then, as a macabre joke, to finish off the crucifixion, Manuel had fashioned a multi-stranded coil and forced it down on to the farmer's head like a crown of thorns.

"Which bastard did this to ya?" growled Zach as he swung down from the saddle and moved in close, checking to work out a way of removing the spiked wire with the least pain and damage to Josh.

"One o' the Double D crowd," the nester managed to say. "The Mex; the greaser they called Manuel. But it was Bronco who pistol-whipped me in the first place. Then he told the

Mex an' a smart-mouthed kid what t' do." He caught his breath and winced as Zach tried to remove the crown of spikes.

"Sorry fella, these barbs, they're stickin' like fishhooks every which way. You're bleedin' like a stuck pig. It's gonna be painful but there ain't no other way."

"I know that," the farmer tried to joke. "I'm on this side of the wire."

Lo Ming, having been searching around on the ground, had found the hammer and a pair of pincers that Josh had been using before the attack. As Zach worked on the wire with his fingers, he pulled out the staples from the fence posts.

"Don't hurry boys," gasped the dirt farmer, attempting another grin. "I think I'll be stickin' around here all day."

Hoof beats approaching from the direction of the homestead caused Zach to turn his attention away from the job in hand for a moment.

"Your daughter," he told the still imprisoned man.

"Oh hell," Josh Naylor groaned. "Now she's gonna shoot her mouth at me. Can't a man suffer in peace?"

* * *

The dying sun headed down, causing the distant western hills to glow orange as Zach and the others, all weary, finally reached the comfort of the adobe homestead.

"I swear, I don't ever want t' see another single inch of barbed wire on this place again," groaned Ellie. "No sir, not one inch. It just ain't worth the hassle."

"Well you're gonna be mighty disappointed, girl. 'Cos t'morrow I'm orderin' some more from the mercantile. So there."

"Ain't you had enough, Pa? Are ya just plum loco or somethin'?" Ellie's eyes blazed. "They came close t' killin' ya." She turned to Zach and Lo Ming

37

hoping for their support.

Lo Ming's features betrayed nothing of his thoughts. Zach shrugged his shoulders and looked her straight in the eye.

"Your pa's right. If he gives in to scum like them, then life won't be worth a plugged nickel. If he's gonna back down, he might as well just pack up and clear out now."

"That's easy for you t' say, mister," she flared up at him. "You can just saddle up an' high-tail it away from here any time ya like. But what you see when ya look around you in here, that's all we got . . . that and a bit of land."

"Ouch!" her father exclaimed. "You're supposed to be bathin' my back, not tryin' t' skin me."

"Sorry Pa," she sighed then bit her bottom lip. "Guess I got carried away."

"An' don't you go givin' Zach an' Lo Ming a hard time," the homesteader went on to remind her. "They're on our side. Remember?"

Ellie rinsed out the blood-stained cloth she was using and, as she shook it out again, half turned to their guests. For a second or so she hesitated, then flushed as she apologized.

"I'm sorry, fellas. But it's this bull-headed pa of mine. Sometimes I think he's more trouble than a whole mess of young'uns would be." She resumed dabbing the wounds caused by the barbed wire. "Never knows when he's beaten, that's always been his trouble."

"Your father not beaten!" Lo Ming burst in. He was frowning and clearly angered by the girl's outspoken words. "That's why Boss come here. I tell you. Buggy man will fix things."

Ellie looked up at Zach once more.

"Why? Why should you want to help the likes of us, eh? We ain't rich. We can't pay for a hired gun like you."

"My guns ain't for hire, and neither am I," he growled at her. "Lo Ming asked me to help, so I will. But I'm not promisin' anythin' other than I'll try my damnedest to get the job done."

"Mister." Josh Naylor shoved his daughter's ministering hand away from his shoulder for a moment as he twisted around to look at Zach. "We're beholdin' to yer. Take no note on what that fool gal o' mine said. She's a woman. An' ya knows women . . . all mouth!" He grinned up at his daughter then winked. "But she means well."

★ ★ ★

"You want what?" The town mayor left his seat and walked around his ornate desk to stand looking up at his impassive visitors, clearly taken aback by the request. "You know what you're asking me to do, I suppose?"

"Sure I do." Zach stared back and answered calmly. "I'm a full-growed man. I know my own mind."

The mayor stared at them with suspicion written all over his face. He rubbed at the goatee beard which jerked on the end of his chubby chin each time he spoke. Then he asked another series of questions, trying to get to the bottom of the reason for such a suicidal request.

"You in some sort of trouble?"

"Nope."

"You're wanted in another state?"

"Nope."

The town's leading citizen rubbed at his beard again and began to pace, following the patterns of the carpet, obviously deep in thought.

"It don't pay much as a job. You know that, don't you?"

"Uh-huh." Zach played with his tongue on the inside of his cheek. He wasn't noted for his patience.

"It ain't a popular occupation, leastways, not around here," the mayor warned. "Matter o' fact, nobody wants it."

"I do," Zach stated, then added, "but don't you go thinkin' I'm gonna be kissin' anybody's arse t' get it . . . 'cos I ain't!"

41

That did it. The mayor turned on his heel and marched to his desk, then rummaged around in one of the drawers. He produced a well-thumbed leather-bound Bible and held it out to Zach.

"Place your left hand on the good book, raise your right arm, state your name then swear after me . . . "

\* \* \*

Two minutes later Zach and Lo Ming were back on the night street again, but this time things were different. They were making a beeline for the jailhouse and law office.

There was no need for Zach to use the key that the mayor had given him. The door of the law office swung open to a gentle push and a smoky oil lamp shed a yellow light inside the room. When they stepped inside, the noise of loud snoring came to them from behind another open doorway at the rear of the office.

42

The two looked at each other, shrugged and, with Zach leading the way, went on to investigate the source of the noise. In one of the three iron-barred cells a pile of rags snorted and grunted at regular intervals.

"Town drunk," Lo Ming explained.

"Not for long, he ain't," grinned the new sheriff as he sorted through his recently acquired bunch of keys, closed the cell door and tried a key in the lock. The key turned and the lock worked with a well-oiled click. Leaving it that way, Zach nodded down at the sleeping drunk. "That's one fella who's gonna have a shock when he wakes up." With that they retreated to the office again. "And t'morrow he'll not be the only one."

"Boss?" Lo Ming said shyly.

"Uh-huh?"

"You forgettin' somethin'?"

Zach tried hard not to grin while he looked around until he found the office Bible.

"Come on then, this is serious

43

business." He tossed the battered volume to the excited Chinaman. "Take the book in your left hand, raise your right hand an' say after me . . . "

# 3

"WHAT in the hell? Hey! Is there anybody out there?" The voice which yelled out from the cell block had more than a hint of panic in it. "Hey, help me somebody. I'm locked in here."

It was close to noon. Zach had sent Lo Ming back home for a couple of hours to check on his horses, and also to make certain that Josh Naylor and his daughter were safe. Zach was busy browsing through the dusty piles of official notices, wanted posters and the law office copy of the town ordnances when his involuntary prisoner's words broke into his thoughts. He grinned. Glad of the interruption, he shut the book with a snap, then yelled back, "Pipe down in there."

For a short time there was a stunned silence before a hesitant, not so loud question came from the cell area.

"Who's that?"

"The sheriff. Who'd ya expect — your momma?" A slightly longer silence followed before the prisoner spoke again.

"We ain't got a sheriff. Hey, whoever y'are, you've had your joke. Be a pal, get me out of here will ya?"

Scraping back his chair noisily on the bare planked floor, Zach got to his feet. Limping a little, he went on through to the cell block. On the other side of the locked, iron-barred door, a bleary-eyed confounded man, in need of a shave and a bath, stared out at him stupidly.

Twisting his face in distaste, the sheriff blew out from between pursed lips, averted his head and stepped back, clear away from the prisoner.

"Fella what in the name of hell kinda booze have ya been drinkin'? That smell o' yours . . . well, to tell the truth, you'd make a skunk sick."

From below a brow, wrinkled with

46

the pain of a hangover, bemused and half-opened bloodshot eyes focused with difficulty on the six-pointed silver star. The eyes blinked then searched upward for Zach's face again.

"Yep, that says 'Sheriff' all right," he said, his frown accentuating at this sudden acquisition of knowledge. "I feel sick. Let me out."

"No can do." Zach grinned as he shook his head. "You're in jug for a month. But if you look, I've put a bucket in the corner behind ya."

"*A month?*" The still inebriated man considered this, then as the words sank in, exploded, "A month?" Two grimy hands suddenly clawed at the iron bars. "But that ain't right. It can't be; I ain't been charged or nothin'." The town drunk was sobering up rapidly. He became truculent and banged ineffectually on the bars with the sides of his fists. "Hey man, don't fool around. You can't keep me here."

Zach laughed and shook his head. As he took down a small blackboard and picked up a chunk of white chalk from the same shelf, he asked, "Good with a gun are yer?"

Alarm showed in the other's face and he was quick to make a reply.

"Yeah — sure I was good with a Colt, better than most, but I ain't ever harmed anyone with a gun in all my natural. There's nobody who can say any different." He flapped his right hand against his side. "See for yourself, I don't even carry a gun any more. Traded it for two jugs o' store liquor — more than a month ago."

"Ya mean, you drink that stuff . . . store liquor? I sure do question your sense of values." Zach tut-tutted, then his eyes changed and he became more business-like. "You were drunk." He got the board and rubbed at it with the palm of his hand. "The law here says you can get from one to thirty days detention for that — at the sheriff's discretion." The grin returned and his alert eyes creased into crows' feet at the edges. "And I'm a son-of-a-bitch sheriff. Right?" The chalk was poised. "Now son, what's ya name?"

"Name?" Evidently shocked and extremely subdued, the man on the other side of the bars grappled with the question. "Oh, er, Ray Jackson." Perplexed, he watched his captor scrawl his name, and cringed at the screeching of the chalk on the board. "What's the big idea?" he asked. "Why arrest me? Believe me, I ain't ever done wrong." These latter words were almost shouted as a sudden anger bubbled up. Then he controlled himself, and took a deep breath, closing his eyes against the throbbing headache of his hangover. Dropping his voice, he changed his tune. "Ah, come on, you don't mean it. Be reasonable, give me a break."

"You broke the law. As for arrestin' ya. You crawled in here on your ownsome, an' did that yourself."

"But I can't stay in jail for thirty days. I'll go plum crazy, sittin' in here, doin' nothin'."

The sheriff smiled.

49

"Don't you worry none on that score. You won't go crazy son. You're gonna work for your keep." He looked around at the cell area. "Yes, sir, this old jailhouse an' my office, you can see they're sorely in need of a real good clean-up an' a lick o'paint." Turning his attention back to the prisoner he asked as an afterthought, You hungry?"

"Famished," Ray Jackson admitted freely. "I could eat a scabby steer if it was covered in maggots."

"Good . . . do some work an' you'll get ya vittles." Pushing the key into the lock of the cell door, Zach paused before turning it. Arching his expressive eyebrows, he spoke brusquely. "Well, it's make-your-mind-up time. What's it gonna be — work or good old starvation?"

"That ain't fair. I ain't even been given the chance t' pay a fine."

"Got any money?"

"Nope."

"I wish you hadn't said that," Zach groaned. "You just don't have a lot of luck," he went on sadly.

Ray Jackson's worried frown deepened. He swallowed hard then asked, "Why?"

"No cash. That's another thirty days for vagrancy." He withdrew the key and began to walk away, sucking in his cheeks to stop himself smiling, as he replaced the blackboard and chalk. "You an' lady luck seem t' be complete strangers, don't ya boy?"

"Sheriff! Don't leave me locked inside here. I'd sooner work, like ya said." The keys rattled and the lock clicked back.

"Better have a wash, there's a pump out in the yard, but don't try to run for it, or you'll never leave this place." Zach pointed to the back door. "An' when you've done that . . . come in an' grab some coffee an grub."

★ ★ ★

When Lo Ming rode back into town word had already got around that there was a new sheriff. Folks on

51

the boardwalks stood and watched the diminutive deputy pass them by.

"You given up horse ranchin' to be the new sheriff?" the blacksmith asked, looking up from the red-hot shoe he was forming on his anvil.

"No. Me deputy," Lo Ming answered honestly. Moving along at the same pace, he called back, "Still have ranch."

"Maybe, but that'll not be for long," the blacksmith's waiting customer muttered. "That Chinky's either due for a one-way trip t' Boot Hill, or he'll be moved on out of the territory. Either way, you know as well as me, his place'll end up same as the rest of 'em, owned by Dan Dawson."

"Yeah, pity," the blacksmith sighed, resuming his task. "Kinda liked that little guy. He always paid on the nail. Yes sir, a pretty good customer for a Chinaman."

Ray Jackson, cleaned up and with food in his belly, was sweeping the front porch of the law office when the new deputy dismounted and strolled past him. Zack greeted him from the open doorway. He bent his head to indicate his prisoner.

"That there hard-workin' young fella's Ray Jackson. He's doin' thirty days. Come on in an' take a look-see at what a fine job o' work he's done."

"Sheriff?"

"What ya want, Jackson?"

"Isn't there some way I can get around this thirty days business?"

The sheriff appeared to ponder on the question for a spell. He scratched his head then rubbed at his jaw. When he looked up he spoke with some hesitation. "There sure is. If you have yourself a respectable job to keep you occupied. An' if ya swear on oath t' stay away from that booze you've been swillin' down ya gullet. But it's the job that matters most. Has to have a regular wage, and accommodation to keep you from vagrancy."

"Ah hecky-me, there ain't a soul in this here town who'd give me work, even if there was some."

Winking at Lo Ming, Zach shrugged expressively and sighed. "Now that's too bad. If that's the case I can't see nothin' for ya 'ceptin' a lifetime of moppin', sweepin' jailhouse floors and cleanin' out privies, unless . . . "

"Unless?" The prisoner stopped sweeping. The bright light of hope shone in his eyes as he looked earnestly at the lawman. "Unless what, Sheriff?"

"I could give you a regular job that would fit the bill."

"You'd do that?" Ray Jackson forgot the sweeping and approached the doorway in awe. "You ain't joshin' me?"

"I guess I'd risk it . . . if you'll swear on oath."

"I'll swear, I'll swear." Ray was wreathed in smiles. "Sheriff I'll do any mortal thing sooner than spend time behind the bars of them there cells."

* ★ ★

"You cheated me," Ray declared as the three of them rode out to head for the Double D range. "I should "ave knowed there was a catch in it when you said you had a job."

"Well it ain't no use belly-achin' t' me, son," Zach grinned back at him. "You had the choice. Nobody forced ya."

"Deputy — good job," Lo Ming advised the latest recruit to their ranks. "Better than jail."

"I wouldn't get shot at in jail, would I, eh?"

"Everybody has to die sometime," the sheriff pointed out. "Hell, it ain't so bad, wearin' a star. At least ya can sleep nights . . . providin' you're not on duty."

When the trio calmly trotted their mounts up to the front steps of the impressive ranch-house, the hands gathered around with interest.

"Where's Dawson?" Zach went

straight to the point.

"He's away again, for the next couple o' days," old Abe told them. "But don't ask where, he don't tell anyone that . . . ever."

"You shut that mouth o' yours." It was Bronco's voice, and came from the sheriff's left. "Where the boss goes has nothin' to do with anyone else." The ranch foreman came closer, the rowels of his Mexican spurs jingling as, hands on hips, he swaggered along the veranda. Then he stopped and a smile of amusement spread over his face. He pointed. "Look boys, the good Lord's sent us another sheriff . . . and two brand new deputies. A drunk an' the Chink from the horse ranch."

Zach moved his horse a couple of steps further ahead of his men, giving himself clear vision on either side.

"I want you Bronco." His words were loud and clear for all to hear and understand.

Bronco's smile vanished. His eyes darted around at his own men, willing them to back his play if they were needed.

"You're mighty sure of yourself, stranger. This ain't like back in town. You're not comin' up on us from behind. If you try pushin' your luck here, mister, you're dog-meat."

"Drop your gunbelt." A murmur of anticipation swelled up from the ranchhands, but Zach sat his horse and never took his eyes off Bronco. He knew he could rely on Lo Ming to cover his back, but was uncertain of Ray.

"Make me!" Bronco Parks snarled back as he crouched, elbow curved stiffly out from his body. The extended fingers of his hand trembled, ready and eager to grab the butt of his .45 Peacemaker and whip it from its holster.

Zach's hand looked no more than a blur. At the same time an ominous audible click told every watcher, and the challenger, that a pistol was drawn, cocked and already aimed steadily at the centre of the ranch foreman's chest.

The colour drained from Bronco's features. He stood as if petrified, saying nothing, hardly breathing, his eyes focused on the sheriff's hand-gun.

"Drop ya belt, or go for it," was all Zach offered, and as though mesmerized, the other man obeyed. Gingerly, feeling with his left hand, the gunbelt was unbuckled and permitted to slip to the boards of the veranda with a dull thud.

"Sheriff . . . you're as good as dead," Bronco warned, still trying to bluff it out in front of his men. "Dan Dawson don't ever let his boys get pushed around, not by the law or anyone. He'll be mad as hell if ya take me in, and that tin star you're wearin's not gonna save ya hide. He ain't the kind t' take this lyin' down."

Laughing, Zach motioned the unarmed man away from the fallen gunbelt. "Fella, I'm shakin' in my boots." He glanced around at the others standing sullenly, covered by the guns of the deputies. "Now where's this Mexican who plays around with barbed wire? And I want his side-kick, the kid from Kansas." Nobody moved or offered to tell. His gaze picked out then settled on Abe once more. "Well, old man. Where are they?"

Before answering, Abe drew the last puff of smoke from his cigarette, then flicked the spittle-wet butt in an arc towards the horse trough. He shrugged his angular shoulders to show his disinterest.

"Who knows? I sure as hell don't. Can't say's I care much either."

"For an oldtimer," Zach noted drily, "you seem to go out of your way, not to know a lot."

"That may be. But I'm still alive, Sheriff," Abe answered slyly. "Now ain't that the truth, eh?"

For a brief moment before Zach dismounted, his eyes met and held the old man's. Neither man flinched. Each of them respected and understood the other, almost like friends.

"Keep your eyes peeled," Zach cautioned his deputies. "If anyone twitches an eyebrow, let him have it where it hurts." With that he limped towards the ranch foreman, kicking the discarded gunbelt further along the veranda out of temptation's way. Then stony-faced, he snapped a pair of new-fangled manacles on to his prisoner's powerful wrists. He gave him a shove towards the steps. "Which is your horse?"

Still acting tough in front of his minions, Bronco swaggered up to his gelding.

"The best of 'em," he boasted, tightening the girth with a savage, jerking heave. "You don't think I'd ride a bag o'bones like these other fellas, do ya?"

"Mount up, and be thankful you ain't been tied belly-down across the saddle."

"There's a gun drawin' a bead on your back, Sheriff."

Zach felt a tingle of fear ripple up his

spine as he heard old Abe's warning.

"Where?" he asked as calmly as he could, without turning or altering his direction.

"Top winda . . . in the centre," Abe added out of the side of his mouth.

"Thanks — I owe you one." Zach took two more steps, then went into action. As he dropped down to one knee, a bullet from a carbine whined close over his head and kicked up dust. Simultaneously he whipped out his .45, and thumbing back the hammer, squeezed the trigger, aiming at the window where the shot had come from.

Glass clattered from the frame and Zach saw the curtains flapping as splinters of bullet-chopped wood tore through them. More bullets dug the earth around him and he suddenly felt lonely.

"Shoot the bastard, Kansas," Bronco screamed as he sat his bucking mount while the rest of his men dived for cover. "Kill 'im."

All at once the boom of Lo Ming's

shotgun Showdown sounded like a clap of thunder on doomsday. The curtains in the window appeared to blow in with a breeze, then fell back. There was no more gunfire.

"You stupid old bastard," Bronco cursed the oldtimer. "You'll pay for that. I'll get you for what you just did. Jesus . . . ya helped a lawman. I could 'ave been free now."

"You two stay here," Zach yelled to his deputies. His limp forgotten along with his normal pain, he ran, crouching low, to the front door of the house. With his heart thudding fit to smash his ribs, he flattened himself against the wall until he had reloaded his Colts. Ready again, he made his way inside.

It was darker, cooler and quieter inside the well-furnished ranch-house. Beads of perspiration gathered on Zach's face, formed into tiny rivulets, then trickled continuously down his neck to his chest. Each time he moved, his sweat-soaked shirt dragged as it stuck to his hot skin.

From somewhere in the house, a door banged repeatedly, caused, Zach surmised, by the draught coming from the shattered window upstairs. His breathing was deafening to his ears. He fought to control it, lest it should give him away. He waited, listening for the slightest sound of a creaking floorboard, or any movement at all from the rooms directly above him. Each and every second expanded into hours within his expectant mind. He had an almost uncontrollable urge to fling caution to the wind, charge up the staircase and get the job over with. But he knew better.

One at a time he wiped his palms dry on the seat of his pants then, hefting a pistol in each fist, stealthily sidled to the bottom of the stairs. Slowly he ascended, careful to test each step in case it should squeak. There was every chance that the backshooter was wounded if not already dead. Zach realized that, but on the other hand, the assassin could be there, around the next corner, or in a doorway, waiting, with his eager finger on the trigger.

The smell that met his nostrils was heavy, and offensively pungent. *The dirty bastard's farted,* he thought. Then he grinned. *Either that, or he knows I'm gunnin' for 'im and he's made one hell of a mess in his pants.*

The stench came to him on the gentle breeze which cooled the sweat on his left cheek as he stood on the top stair. *Well fella, you ain't dead yet — but you're gonna be,* Zach promised in a mental note as he edged his head around the bannister. The landing was empty, apart from, on one wall, a half-moon walnut table with a bowl of gaudy wax fruits on its polished surface. At the far end, a curtained window let in the sunlight. On each side of the passage were two doors. All except one, were wide open.

"Hey . . . bushwhacker! I'm comin' for ya," he called out, his voice taunting, planned to spook Kansas. Zach held the .45s ready and trained towards the open doors. "Have ya ever been shot, boy? It hurts. Yeah, burns like a red-hot poker goin' into ya."

A loud fart reverberated inside the room furthest away from him, on the left.

"If I was a gamblin' man I'd wager a month's pay that you're gettin' more than a mite worried," the lawman suggested. Then he altered his tone. "Be sensible fella. Toss your gun out on to the landin', then come out with your hands up."

"You think I'm dumb or somethin'?" Kansas shouted back. "There's only one guy who's worried around here, an' it ain't me, mister."

"Hero, eh?" Zach shouted back his reply. "Well, heroes die like anyone else." His anger began to ebb and he felt a sense of sorrow for the lad holed up in the bedroom. "Do yourself a favour boy. Dyin' ain't nice. Give in before it's too late . . . ya don't have t' throw yer life away, not for the likes of Bronco."

There was a pause until Kansas asked, "Can I trust you? I mean, you wouldn't lie t' me. Would ya?"

"Son, I give you my word. An' I ain't ever broken that in the whole of my life. Believe me."

From the far bedroom doorway a Winchester carbine suddenly flew out and clattered on the floor. Zach let out a sigh of relief.

"You're showin' good sense, boy. Now come out nice an' easy with both your hands reachin' high."

"Kansas . . . kill the bastard!" The unmistakable voice of the ranch foreman could be heard yelling from outside. "Kill 'im. It's your only chance, boy."

Christ! raged Zach, under his breath. That's put the wolf in the sheep pen.

"Don't listen to Bronco, son. He'll get you killed if ya . . . "

The sheriff's plea was too late. In a frenzied flurry of movement, Kansas dived out from the bedroom doorway, grabbed the Winchester and began to spray bullets blindly towards the staircase as he stood up.

Zach had no choice. The trigger fingers on each hand squeezed at the same instant. His matched Colts bucked hard as they fired together.

With his chest smashed in by the heavy calibre, snub-nosed bullets, Kansas Smith seemed to fly, flung back like a rag doll. There was a crash as glass shattered and splintered then he disappeared through the window.

"Jesus," sighed Zach, already getting to his feet as he heard the body smash on to the sun-baked boards of the veranda. Angrily kicking the discarded Winchester aside, he peered sadly from the broken window. Below, wrapped in the curtains which had dragged out with him, Kansas was already wearing his shroud. "Poor young bastard."

67

# 4

"**Y**OU'D better come along with us, oldtimer," Zach suggested casually as he watched two of the ranchhands wrapping a shiny yellow slicker around the battered body of Kansas Smith and roping it securely to the back of his horse. "I can't see it bein' too healthy for you to stay around here after we've gone."

Abe pushed his leather tobacco sack back into his shirt pocket, licked the edge of the cigarette he was rolling, then twisted it into shape and smoothed it down as he thought over the offer.

"Seems like good advice t' me, Sheriff." He paused and looked around at the other ranchhands. None of them had said anything since his warning had saved Zach's life, but whenever they had looked at him there had been the gleam of hate in their eyes. To them, he

68

was a traitor and they had only one way of dealing with those. "Yeah, I guess the boys around here ain't plannin' on votin' me in as president of the local glee club." He grinned wryly.

Zach nodded his understanding of the situation. There was something he liked about the old man. When he spoke again his voice was low and confidential.

"Don't ya feel you're too damned old for this kind of game?" he asked.

"Uh-huh. I know I'm too long in the tooth for this stuff. I was plannin' on movin' along anyhow." He struck a match and as it flared, went on. "But it was a job." As he lit his roll-up, puffed a couple of times then exhaled with a grateful sigh, he gave an explanation. "Earnin' a livin' don't come easy at my age, son." He stopped, thinking for a moment, then gave a derisive laugh. "Huh . . . livin'! But I've come to the fork in the trail here. I couldn't stomach any more of what's been goin' on with this outfit. What they did t' that nester, with the barbed wire, was enough to put me off."

"Go get your things together, we'll hang on for a few minutes 'til you get back," Zach confirmed to put the old man's mind at rest. "But shake the lead out, will ya?"

Zach had hardly settled in his saddle when Abe came hurrying back with a gunny sack slung over his shoulder and a pair of well-scuffed saddle-bags swinging from the crook of his arm.

"I'm ready, Sheriff," he stated, hooking the gunny sack on the horn of his saddle and swinging the saddle-bags in place across his horse in double quick time. "Don't let me hold the party up for you younger fellas." With that he mounted up and neck-reined his cow pony around to face the trail into town.

* * *

As they entered the sheriff's office, Bronco uttered yet another threat.

"You're dead. All of ya." Then he stabbed his finger viciously towards Abe. "And you," he shouted. "There ain't a hole anywhere in this territory that's deep enough for ya to crawl in. You'll not even make it to Boot Hill. The boss'll send the Mex after ya. He'll hunt you down an' slit ya into little strips of jerky, then feed ya to the dogs — that's how you'll end up. An' you'll finish up the same, Sheriff, if ya don't get religion an' come to your senses."

Zach wore a pained expression as he pushed his prisoner hard in the back to propel him through the doorway leading to the cells.

"Why don't you give that big overworked mouth of yours a rest, Bronco? It's a wonder you ain't worn them lips of yours down t' yer chin." He reached up and unhooked a bunch of keys from a nail on the wall, looked at Ray Jackson and jerked his head as he tossed him the keys. "Lock 'im up Ray — and lock 'im up good. We don't want to lose this one."

71

"Ya know somethin'," Abe remarked sarcastically, "I've always had a funny feelin' that Bronco didn't like me. Now I know."

"Want a job?" Zach cut in suddenly.

"Me . . . a job . . . here?" Abe acted astounded. "Why me?"

"You're all that's available."

"Oh." Abe mused for a second, then spoke out loud. "That means I'm kinda indispensable then, don't it?"

"No," Zach growled. "Do you want the job or not?"

"Well, if ya put it like that. Yeah, I'll take it."

The sheriff caught Lo Ming's attention and indicated the desk as he spoke.

"Pass me that old Bible out of that top drawer, will you?" He slapped Abe on the shoulder and winked. "I've got me another deputy."

* * *

Word soon got out on to the street that the new sheriff had shot and killed one of the men at the Double D ranch. What intrigued the townsfolk more, was the fact that he had dared to arrest the ranch foreman. Not only that, but he was actually holding him in the jailhouse to await the next visit of the circuit judge. The judge was not due for close on a month . . . and everyone knew an awful lot could happen inside a month.

Excited speculation grew as it passed on through the town, like canned beans through a skeleton. For the next three days the main topic of conversation was, how long would it be before Dan Dawson returned from wherever he was? That, most folks estimated, was how long the careers and lives of the newly-appointed lawmen would last. Dawson would put the pressure on and never back down. If the new sheriff was of a like mind, there was bound to be plenty of shooting and killing, same as in a regular war. Even the Baptist preacher at the mission would bet on that.

If Zach was worried, he certainly did not show it to anyone. Confidently and calmly he went about his duties, dealing with the normal day-to-day contingencies of his office, yet staying continually on the alert. All this time he devised plans ready for the return of the Double D's owner.

At some time each day Zach and one of his deputies would make a point of riding out to call and see how the nester was recovering. At the same time, the keen-eyed Ellie would keep him informed of anything she spotted happening on the other side of the fence, on the Double D land. She was a bright girl and did not miss much, especially while checking for signs of more trouble around the holding.

"You make good an' sure you keep them guns loaded, and handy to get at durin' the next week or two," Zach had warned Josh Naylor during one such visit. "Better show that gal of yours how to load an' shoot one too."

Josh had gaped in disbelief.

"Hell, Sheriff, my Ellie can shoot the pip out of a peach at nigh on a hundred yards. I tell ya, that gal's a sight better with a rifle than me." He had looked and pointed at a framed picture on the mantelshelf that showed a woman not much older than Ellie. "That there's her momma. Ellie's a lot like her. Yeah, 'til the day she died, that woman o' mine, she could always go out with a gun and bring plenty of good vittles home. Yes sir, anythin' from a mess of fat squirrels, to a full grown whitetail stag."

For a while it had been as though Josh's mind was back in the distant past. When he had slapped his thighs at a sudden memory, the pain from his wounds had caused him to wince, but he had carried on. "Shot a grizzly once," he'd said proudy. "Biggest damned animal I ever did see."

"Fine lookin' woman," Zach had complimented him. "Reminds me a little of my own, 'ceptin' my wife could never shoot a gun."

"She dead — like mine?"

"Uh-huh."

The shared grief of the memories had united the two men, and they'd understood each other better because of them.

★ ★ ★

"He's back . . . I've seen him," Ellie exclaimed one particular morning before Zach and Lo Ming had time to dismount.

"Dawson?" the sheriff asked, still standing poised on one stirrup. "When — where?" He dismounted and moved in closer listening for her answer, enjoying her nearness.

"This mornin'. Ridin' down that way with a bunch of his boys." As she spoke she pointed her arm downstream, towards the narrow cleft between the distant hills, which funnelled the end of the valley.

"What were they doin', could you

76

see?" Zach persisted. "Think hard, Ellie, it could be real important."

She shook her head so that her hair lashed around her shoulders, bringing back memories to him, stirring his loins.

"They had a couple of pack mules trailin' along with 'em. Loaded with boxes but I couldn't tell what was inside. As to what they were intendin' on doin', I've no idea, but I'd give you odds they weren't out for no picnic."

A sudden tumble of explosions sounded like distant thunder. The noise came to them in waves from the direction of the hills, downstream.

"Blasting powder," Lo Ming announced positively. "Same like me use on railways."

"Now what in the hell would a cattle spread be usin' explosives for?" Zach wondered out aloud.

"I don't know and I sure don't care," Ellie affirmed. "Just as long as he leaves us alone, I ain't gonna worry if he sticks 'em all in his ear and blows his brains out."

"If that blastin' had been upstream," the sheriff reasoned, "maybe you'd have had cause to worry."

She gave him a quizzical look.

"Why's that?"

"Dawson could cut water supply," Lo Ming announced. "Without water . . . your farm . . . my horses." He shrugged and expressed himself with open hands. "Everything die."

* * *

The sun had barely had time to drop out of sight beyond the horizon when there was the drumming of horses' hooves coming towards the sheriff's office.

"Lo Ming think you right, Boss," the Chinese deputy remarked, crossing to peer out of the window.

"Yeah, that's them," old Abe agreed, instinctively easing his hand-gun in its holster as he looked out over the top

78

of Lo Ming's head. "That's Dawson comin' in to throw his weight about and show the town how he can spring his top hand from jail."

"Then he's in for a surprise, ain't he?" Zach pointed out as he buckled on his gunbelt and made for the door. "He's gonna learn the time for throwin' his weight around is over an' done with."

The thunder of hooves came to a halt amidst a cloud of dust which billowed up outside the windows. Men's voices shouted and laughed, and noisy footsteps clumped determinedly on the boardwalk leading to the office.

The door burst open, shaking with the ferocity of force which had been applied to it by the man who barged inside. He stopped dead, then stepped back against those who would have followed him in.

A hand, large and powerful shoved with relentless determination against the big rancher's chest, propelling him backwards like he did not matter.

"Out," Zach told him curtly. "Nobody comes into my office like they own it, except me. Savvy, fella?"

"Just who in the hell," began the ousted man with red-faced anger fit to boil over. "D'you know who you're tryin' to push around?"

Immediately, the rowdy followers behind him stopped their banter and, electrified by the tension between their boss and the new lawman, lapsed into an expectant silence.

The sheriff eyed the other with no display of emotion. He stroked at his jaw thoughtfully for a time before he spoke.

"Yeah, big an' ugly. Fancy clothes. Mean eyes and a loud mouth . . . yes, I reckon I know who you are. You're the piece of horse shit who thinks he owns this town." He stepped forward and pushed again at the belligerent rancher so that he was forced to step back off the boardwalk and on to the dirt road. "Well for your information, Dawson," he growled, "there ain't anyone round here who can own me — or my men. Understand?"

"Ha!" Dan Dawson retorted. Then he snarled, twisting his mean lips to one side, revealing a flash of gold teeth. "That was what the last sheriff of this burg said. Now look where he is."

Taking a further short step forward towards the rancher, Zach raised his eyebrows and, as he spoke, lowered his voice so that his words had all the coldness of ice.

"That some sort of a threat, Dawson? You callin' me out, eh?"

An excited murmur went up from the men behind Dawson. Their boss had never been challenged like that before. They waited, wondering.

"I don't indulge in street brawls, Sheriff. It ain't my style. I came to get my foreman out of jail." Reaching inside his jacket he pulled out a bulging leather wallet, and opened it wide. Everyone around him could see it was stuffed with high denomination dollar bills. "I need Bronco at the ranch so I've come to pay his fine."

"He ain't been fined, only charged," Zach confirmed.

"Well then, in that case" — Dawson suddenly grinned and pulled out a wad of bills from the wallet and held them toward the sheriff — "it's no problem then, is it? Here, this should more than pay for his stay in your custody."

Zach's eyes gazed with disgust into the other's face and watched the smile fade away to a pale-faced nothing of an expression.

"You get your damned arse out of here, and take that bunch of mangy coyotes along with you, before I arrest you for attemptin' to bribe an officer of the law." He pushed hard and Dawson all but fell, only saving himself from doing so by grabbing for support from one of his men.

He said no more until he was safely mounted with others between him and the lawman.

"You've not heard the last of this, Zach Scott," he warned as he wheeled his horse to face the other way. "Why should I soil my hands on the likes of you when I pay others to clean up horse shit?" With that said, he kicked his mount into motion and sped away at the gallop. Behind him trailed his men, surprised by his vulnerability.

"He'll be back, like he said," Abe affirmed from a yard behind Zach. "Maybe not himself in flesh, but it'll be some fella with an easy trigger finger and the need for a fast buck. You can count on it."

"That's for sure, Sheriff," Ray Jackson added. "Dan Dawson won't enjoy bein' shown up in front of his crew. You'd better keep out of the shadows and watch your back from now on."

"We all watch your back," Lo Ming stated. "Take turns. See you safe . . . OK?"

"And you can all go t' hell. I ain't ever been namby-pambied in all my natural, and I sure as hell don't intend

to be now. No sir, you fellas look out
for yourselves an' I'll do the self-same
thing right?"

* * *

Checking the money he had withdrawn
from his own more than adequate
account as he came out of the bank next
morning, Zach stopped and ducked
back into the shadow of the doorway.
He had happened to notice one of the
Double D ranchhands emerging from
the telegraph office further along the
same block. The cowpoke was up
to no good, acting furtively and
avoiding passers-by. Pulling his hat
brim down to shield his face, he
climbed into the saddle of his cattle
pony then waited, checking around
before moving away from the hitch
rail. Only when sure he was not being
observed, did he head out of town
. . . by a backroad.

Stuffing the cash into his trouser
pocket, Zach marched along and entered

the telegraph office.

"Yeah?" asked the clerk barely raising his eyes from the newspaper he was reading. "Fill out a message on the pad an' I'll send it later, as soon as the line's free."

"Never mind later. I want you here. Now!" With that the sheriff slapped his hand loudly on the green-painted counter top, causing the inkwell to bounce and splash black ink all over the surface of the paper pad.

The news sheet was discarded and the clerk responded like a trained dog, ready to wag his tail or do any damned thing he was asked.

"Yes sir, Sheriff. Anythin' you say, Sheriff. What can I do for you, eh? Just you name it."

"The last fella who came in here. I want to see what he sent."

The clerk lifted his eyeshade higher and gawped across the counter at Zach.

"But I can't do that," he gasped, horrified by the idea of such a request. "It ain't ethical. Everythin' I send over the wire's private, and strictly confidential. That's company policy. Always has been."

"Cut the bullshit. I'm the sheriff. Let me see what I've asked for, or so help me, I'll have you behind bars for obstructin' me in the line o' my duty, so damned fast you'll think you've been a parrot all of your life."

"But I haven't sent it yet. Like I said, the wire's still busy." The telegraphist squirmed, uncertain what he should do. Zach told him.

"Then, little man," he said, reaching over and grasping hold of his narrow shoulder to pull him hard up against the edge of the counter. "Show me what he wants you to send."

"All right Sheriff, as long as it's official business, I guess you've a right to know." His slender-fingered hand slipped under the counter. "But I can't give it into your hands. It's more than my job's worth." Bringing out a clip-board, he held it within reading distance but not the reach of Zach.

"You know how it is, when folks have to trust you."

But Zach wasn't listening, he was too interested in the message and what it could mean to him.

# 5

"**B**OSS, Boss," Lo Ming yelled excitedly as he galloped up to the sheriff's office. Hauling hard on the reins he leaned back and skidded his sweating horse to a dust-raising halt. Then, leaping from the saddle he ran the last few steps to where he saw Zach already waiting in the shade of the office door.

"Hey, slow down a mite," the sheriff suggested with a grin. "What's the commotion about? Is yer arse on fire?"

"The Naylors . . . land . . . house," the Chinaman gasped. "All under water."

"Flooded? Anybody hurt? Is the girl all right?" Zach asked. As the winded Chinese deputy gasped and shook his head to the first question, then nodded for the second, he continued. "How'd it happen? There ain't been no rain storms or nothin'."

"The creek. Backed up. Overflowed banks."

"I should've known." Zach smashed one of his fists into the palm of his other hand. "Dawson! Those explosions we heard, downstream." As he turned back into his office his anger showed clearly on his face. "Damn him. That sneaky, low-down, snake in the grass," he retorted angrily. "Dawson wasn't gonna dry 'em out. That would've been too slow for him. Oh no, he wanted it done the quick way. His aim was to wash 'em out." Already he was putting on his hat and drawing on his riding gloves. He looked at Lo Ming. "Where are the Naylors now?"

"My place. I take them there. They safe. Land much higher than Naylor's. Water not reach."

"Well that's a mercy," Zach grunted thoughtfully. For a while he stood, head down with his chin cradled in his hand, thinking. Suddenly he straightened up and his eyes glittered with determination. "Right, this is what we're gonna do. Now listen to what I'm gonna tell yer. And listen good."

★ ★ ★

As they moved along, the sheriff and his three deputies gazed down from high up on Lo Ming's ranch. Below them, a newly formed narrow lake filled most of the lower part of the valley. The water stretched in a continuous sheet into the distance, silent and still. Sadly, stranded like an island, was the roof of Josh Naylor's home with its now smokeless chimney-stack pointing like a finger at the sky. It was all that remained to remind Zach and his men that, mere hours earlier, a well-run farm had existed.

"Even if the water goes," Ray Jackson remarked, "I don't think old Josh'll get any kind of crop. At least, not this year."

Zach clicked his tongue at his buggy horse and tickled its back with the whip

90

to send the animal into a steady but faster gait towards the far end of the valley. "And he won't get a crop next year neither," he declared, "unless we stop gabbin' an' get a move on."

Lo Ming and Ray Jackson heeled their ponies to stay abreast of the buggy.

"Think that stuff'll do the trick, Sheriff?" Ray asked doubtfully, looking down at the wooden boxes in the back of the buggy. "It don't look much t'me."

"I don't know," Zach admitted honestly. "Accordin' to the storekeeper, it's the latest thing in explosives. He swears it leaves old-fashioned blastin' powder way back in history. Showed me some government report on the stuff . . . seems t' be good."

"Black powder best," the Chinaman stated sullenly. "Powder used on railways. Lo Ming like best."

"Well we ain't got any," Zach almost snapped back. "I tried, but it seems Dan Dawson had the same idea. He bought all there was. We'll have to use what we've got. So that's that!"

At that self-same moment Ray called out.

"Take a look over there, Sheriff we're bein' watched."

The other two looked over to the direction in which his arm pointed. On the Double D side of the new lake a group of riders were working cattle. The cowhands, having spotted the trio, forgot about their job and collected in a tight bunch to discuss and watch. After a minute, one of them broke away from the bunch and, leaving a trail of dust behind him, galloped at full pelt. It was apparent that the cowhand was headed for the ranch-house to inform his boss of what he'd seen.

"Five'll get you ten that fella's not goin' to do us any favours," Ray pointed out. "Somethin' tells me we's in for more than a peck of trouble before this day's through an' done with."

"Yeah," Zach agreed as he goaded

his animal to greater efforts. "But like I've always said, the trouble's free. It goes right along with the job."

The lawmen kept glancing back over their shoulders, checking what was happening. The Double D riders seemed to be doubtful as to what they should do. Then one of them seemed to take on the responsibility for action. With a waving arm he urged the others to follow him. At the same time he turned his cow pony and set off to draw level then keep pace on a parallel track to the lawmen. Within seconds, the others had followed suit and caught him up.

"Told ya we was in for trouble, didn't I, Sheriff?" Ray pointed out smugly.

"Yeah." Zach twisted his face then groaned. "Maybe ya should seek a job tellin' fortunes t' little old ladies back in town," he added with definite irony. After that he lapsed into one of his usual long silences, trying to think ahead and forestall any problems.

All the way along the valley the riders from the Double D shadowed them, staying on station and keeping them in sight, presenting an ever-present threat. Up ahead the hills appeared to grow bigger as they drew closer. The neck of water narrowed as the land steepened on either side and they were forced to let their steeds slow to a walk.

Across the narrowing water, the shadowing riders came closer. By this time it was possible for the officers of the law to recognize the ranchhands' faces, and now and again, even hear their voices.

"You boys had better check yer guns," Zach cautioned, as he nodded up ahead. "If I'm not mistaken, that there cliff on the Double D side, it's juttin' right out into the water. It's gonna put a stop on them fellas. They'll not be able to get much further. Could be they might decide on a showdown an' try to stop us."

Across from them, the leaderless riders looked concerned. They argued among themselves and a couple of them took out their hand-guns to wave them about and shout angrily at each other as though they were ready to use them. Reaching the foot of the cliff they stopped. Some dismounted and stood undecided by their horses. Others dispersed and ran to seek cover behind some low outcrops of sandstone rock beside the water's edge to peek out at the buggy and the two riders on the opposite bank.

The buggy man and his escorts each heaved huge audible sighs of relief as they moved out of sight and range of the Double D bunch, around the corner of the cliff. Grinning broadly, Zach pushed his hat to the back of his head and mopped his brow with his shirt-sleeve.

"Well," he said, "when the chips were down, those Double D boys just couldn't cut the mustard."

"Well, I sure ain't sorry about that," Ray was quick to inform him. "I never pretended I wanted to be the target in someone else's range war."

The water was blocked by a gigantic wall of tumbled rock. On either side of the narrow gulch the cliff faces had been blasted down to block the channel between them.

"Holy cow!" Zach gasped out loud, disappointed by the daunting sight.

"Jesus Christ," Ray Jackson breathed with awe. "That rock pile ain't ever gonna be shifted from there. No sir . . . not in a coon's age."

"Much blasting powder needed for that," Lo Ming said in his amazement. Shaking his head slowly, he noisily sucked in air through his teeth as he went on to explain further, "Many, many pounds of powder. Plenty-much work."

As soon as they reached the makeshift dam, all three dismounted then clambered up and over to view the other, dry side of it.

The agile Chinaman scuttled all over the place, jumping from rock to rock, checking, sighting, making calculations while the white men waited, wondering what he had up his sleeve.

At last Lo Ming seemed to arrive at a conclusion and came to stand stern-faced in front of the sheriff.

"Boss," he said respectfully, giving his normal slight bow of his head, "it is possible to free most of the water."

"What d'ya mean . . . most?" Zach asked. "Will Naylor's land stay flooded, or won't it, eh?"

Lo Ming stood up to his full height and pointed back up the valley. Then with a grand gesture, he swept his arm down again, describing with his hand as he spoke.

"Water all way down here . . . same like normal." His extended finger scribed an arc delicately in the air. "This place," — he pointed to an area around the base of the cliffs — "stay like small, very deep, lake." Then with a sigh which bordered on despair, he added, "Need black powder. Lo Ming understand black powder. Don't know dynamite stuff."

"Well, we ain't got any damned powder," Zach snapped. "So it's no use you or anyone else belly-achin'. We'll just have to do the best we can with this modern stuff." Without waiting for any counter argument, he turned heel and limped his way back to the buggy. "Come on you fellas, let's get this stuff unloaded and taken over to where it's gonna do some good."

It had been scorching work on the dry side of the dam. In among the sun-baked rocks it felt hotter than an oven in hell. Their shirts, soaked in sweat, clung to them like second skins, dragging and hampering their movements as they toiled.

Because of his expert knowledge gained through handling explosives for a railway company, Lo Ming supervised the whole operation. As Lo Ming unrolled the last reel of fuse, Zach and Ray packed the remaining bundles of already primed and fused-up dynamite into the holes the Chinaman had chosen. Then, as he had instructed

98

them, they carefully packed the holes with clay and tamped them tightly with flat-ended wooden poles.

"Four boxes used," Ray remarked. "Never thought we'd ever get to the end of it." Rolling the last of the clay in between his hands, he pushed it into the hole ready for the sheriff. "Don't fancy our chances much if this lot goes up while we're still around."

Zach grinned broadly as he wiped the perspiration from his face before pushing the clay home with his pole then tamping it in tight to form a seal.

"If this lot goes up, that's exactly where we'll be . . . around! There won't be enough left of the three of us to bury in a cigar box."

The sharp crack of an explosion caused their hearts to somersault then beat like an army side-drummer giving a roll. Rock splintered and spattered close to Ray's left ear and he let out an involuntary yelp of fright.

As one, they all dived down behind

whatever cover was at hand, then waited. When no more shots came their way Zach, prudently keeping his head down, called out to his men.

"Seems like that mangy bunch who followed us have made their way around by the long trail." After that he asked, "Everyone all right?" As he spoke, he was already hefting his right-hand pistol in his fist.

"Sure, Boss," the Chinese deputy answered from a yard or two lower down. "How you?"

"Me? Fine. Just dandy." Turning, Zach looked around for the other deputy. "Ray . . . you're not hurt none, are ya, son?"

"Only my pride," the ex-town drunk explained. "Gee, my guts are cryin' out for a swig of red-eye," he admitted sheepishly as he eased out from around the end of the same rock which Zach was hiding behind. "Thought that dynamite stuff had decided to blow. Nearly caused me to have a nasty accident myself . . . in my pants . . . if ya know what I mean."

Working among the sloping jumble of rocks, above them and out of sight, the Chinese explosives expert said nothing. Instead, he worked quietly on, apparently unworried about the possible consequences from the unseen gunman.

Zach took the lid from the last dynamite box, placed his hat on the end and lifted it above the rock behind which he had taken cover. At once a hail of bullets spattered the rocks and he felt the wooden lid buck and splinter in his hands before he had time to withdraw it from view.

"Well there's one thing we know for sure," he muttered as soon as the shooting ceased again. "There's more than one of 'em down there, and they don't act very friendly."

"Me finished, Boss," Lo Ming informed him from overhead. "All ready for plenty big bang."

"Hey! Don't you go lightin' any fuses yet," Ray interjected with more than a hint of alarm in his voice. "We've all got to get to hell out of here first," he pointed out. "An' in case you've not noticed, there's some fellas with guns down there. Fellas who don't aim on lettin' us leave just now."

As though to prove his point, the shooting began again. This time, however, the firing was not so wild and haphazard. Instead it came steady and methodical, designed to keep them all immobilized and with their heads down.

"We can't stay here all night," Ray stated. "I ain't had my vittles, or nothin'."

"Well, boy," Zach told him. "If yer belly's more important than your life, you know where the horses are. To my way o' thinkin' it shouldn't take a young fella like you more'n a spit and a stride, to make it over this pile o' rock to the other side." A bullet zinged off the top of the rock Zach was sheltering behind, then buzzed off into the distance like a mournful bee.

"Don't know how them boys with the guns down there'll take it, you sneakin' away out of their company. No sir, I don't think they'll like it one little bit."

"Hey, you holed-up in the rocks!" someone yelled from down below. "Ain't yer got no fight in yers?"

"Not yet we ain't," Zach joked back without showing himself, "but we're gettin' mighty tired of all that racket yer makin', so we're slowly gettin' round to it."

The shadows were growing longer with each minute that passed and a layer of cloud was spreading across the heavens like a blanket. In another half an hour it would be dark. Unless the moon came out they would no longer be targets for those snipers waiting at the bottom of the dam.

Ray eased himself back around the rock between himself and the sheriff. He grinned and pointed at the sky.

"Cloudin' over and the sun's droppin' like a hawk on to a prairie gopher," he said happily. "Pretty soon we'll be able to stroll out of here without a scratch."

Zach shook his head.

"Stroll? Tell me son, how long d'ya reckon it'll take us to get back up and over the top, back to the horses, eh?"

"Three or four minutes. No more," Ray answered with confidence. Then he appeared to have sudden doubt as Zach's question sank in. "Should be long enough . . . shouldn't it?"

"Three or four minutes?" Zach's tone was acidic. "Over these jumbled rocks — in the dark?"

"Well, supposin' it takes five or even ten minutes," the deputy argued, "what difference will that make?"

The sheriff's jaw set with determination. For a few seconds he grimaced at the younger man, effectively silencing him. Then he raised his voice only enough for the sound to carry up to where the Chinaman sheltered. "Hey, Lo Ming."

"Yes Boss?"

"When ya light them fuses of yours,

how long d'ya reckon we got to skedaddle an' get out of here, before the first explosion?"

"Maybe six minutes . . . maybe four."

Ray looked uncomfortable.

"That ain't too precise, is it fella?" he moaned. "I thought you were supposed to know about explosives an' stuff? Hecky-me, it's our lives you're playin' with."

"Lo Ming not play." He sounded angry. "Me do good job, all same railways."

An even more worried Ray turned to whisper urgently to Zach.

"Hey, Sheriff. You trust that madman?"

"Uh-huh! Always have. And he ain't mad. He's never let me down yet."

Some way further down, a small rock rattled loudly as an unseen foot dislodged it.

Zach risked a quick glance around the side of the boulder and snapped off a shot at the foolhardy cow-poke who scrambled up towards them. The bullet struck home, but only just. The man cried out in his pain, half spun, grabbed at his arm close to the shoulder and fell out of sight among the boulders.

An immediate fusillade of shots came back at them from various points around where the wounded man had disappeared.

"Hey, Sheriff." It was the same sneering voice which had contacted them earlier. "You're all gonna pay for what ya just did t' Clem. You ain't gonna get out of there alive. No sir, none of yers. You ain't goin' nowhere, and fast!"

From time to time the odd shot was fired haphazardly their way. The lawmen just lay back and rested, waiting for the dark to curtain them off from the waiting gunmen.

At last Lo Ming joined them and explained his tactics.

"Boss, you and Ray make way to top of dam. I give you time. Light fuse then come join you."

"No way," Zach told him. You high-tail it out of here. I'll see to the fuses."

"No. You not know where fuses are. You don't know which to light and when. You go first," Lo Ming demanded, patting himself hard on his chest. "My job. Me light fuses. Yes?"

"Well that's fine with me," Ray said gratefully. "I don't aim to take the job away from ya."

Zach thought about it for a time before he made his mind up.

"It makes sense. Yeah, OK Lo Ming, you have it your way, but be careful. We need ya," he explained gruffly. "When we reach the top I'll give you a hoot like an owl. Right?"

As they clambered upwards in to the darkness, Zach mentally counted off the passing seconds. Although there were plenty of hand-holds and places for their feet, finding them took longer than he had expected.

After what Zach estimated to be five minutes they were still little more than two-thirds of the way up. That was when the luck ran out. By pure chance an owl out for an evening's hunting, made a call to its mate. Instantly the flare of a match way down beneath them signalled that Lo Ming had also heard the bird and had already lit the first of the fuses.

"Jesus Christ almighty," Ray exclaimed. "That's done it. The dang fool bird. Come on, Sheriff, or we're dead meat."

The cold hand of fear clutched at Zach and, for a moment he was tempted to shout out a warning to his Chinese friend. But he reasoned that would only draw a storm of gunfire on to the little man. He decided it best to keep quiet and follow his other deputy's example and climb faster.

How long it had taken to reach the top of the dam Zach had no idea. He had forgotten to keep on with the count. Now another worry descended upon him. He could now see his shadow on the rocks. The moon had chosen that particular time to break through and light his way, leaving them exposed as naked targets for anyone with eyes and a gun. As the first of the shots rang out behind him he glanced back at the Chinese deputy. In the moonlight, Lo Ming could be clearly seen, dodging the bullets and leaping from rock to rock, as agile as a young mountain goat, and coming up fast.

Bullets began to strike around Zach and he had to forget his friend and do some dodging on his own account to save his hide. He was no longer clambering upwards but running awkwardly across to where the buggy and horses had been left. As he pressed on over the pile of debris from the cliff faces on either side, he found himself thinking and cussing inwardly. Like a go'damned turkey-shoot . . . an' we're the stupid turkeys. Then he recalled the main reason why he was hurrying. God Almighty, that dynamite stuff. It's liable to blow at any second.

More bullets zipped around Zach as

he lurched from side to side. His mind was in a turmoil of confusion. But there shouldn't be bullets. He could no longer be seen from below. Yet, he could hear the guns. They seemed to be moving closer, and coming from . . . up ahead. When he raised his eyes he saw with utter disbelief the muzzle flashes from among the last line of tumbled rock.

"Steamin' horseshit!" he groaned out aloud, already diving for shelter.

"Bushwhackers, Sheriff," he heard Ray's unnecessary warning shout and became aware that the younger man had already crouched behind cover and was firing ahead to where the shots came from.

Bellying down alongside the deputy, Zach emptied a pistol at their attackers, and as he reloaded from his belt loops, weighed up this new situation. There was only one conclusion he could come to.

"It ain't no use us stayin' here, son," Zach stated. "We're between the devil an' the deep blue sea. And with that new-fangled explosive ready to go up at any second, I reckon we're closer to the devil."

"But Sheriff, we'll get killed out there."

"That's as maybe," Zach answered calmly, grabbing the deputy by his vest and heaving him to his feet as hot lead hummed around them. "Run, an' we might just have an outside chance. Stay, an' we've no chance at all."

# 6

FRIGHTENING! That was the only way to describe it. The ground trembled before it heaved upwards beneath Zach's feet. Ignoring the pains in his legs he ran stumbling over the rocks. A rumble as loud as any thunder he had ever heard, threatened to burst his eardrums and, simultaneously, a hot blast of air struck him in the back with a tremendous force. Unable to resist, he felt himself being lifted bodily and hurled forward like dried-out tumbleweed in a tornado. His chest hit the earth with a bone-shaking bump which drove the air from his body, before he tumbled over and over, finally stopping with his face buried in long, cool, dew-laden grass. As he lay there, gasping for breath, all around him he could hear debris falling, pattering on the ground amid heavier thumps which vibrated his body. From a distance came a roaring such as a gale makes when tearing through a narrow gorge. Merged with this violent maelstrom of sound, the spontaneous cries of terrified men shouting oaths or calling out to their Maker, told their own story.

"Oh God," he muttered from the inflicted pain as a cascade of earth and small stones threatened to beat the life from his body. "It's too late." He said no more. Something hard and heavy struck a glancing blow on his right temple. A momentary, different pain washed over him. What had been a brilliant flash of light was replaced by a velvet darkness relieving him of all further anguish.

★ ★ ★

Zach shivered with cold, yet something warm, moist and gentle tickled at the side of his face. A smell which vaguely reminded him of rotting hay, coupled with a snuffling sound, tested his memory. In his ears was a roaring he could not place, and his head hurt. When he felt tenderly with his fingers there was a wound, swollen and sticky, already crusting with drying blood. He spat out the dirt from his mouth then hesitantly permitted his eyelids to open.

He stared straight up into the quivering nostrils of Lo Ming's horse which stood head down over him, looking and sniffing at his face, while above, a bright silver moon sailed among the patchy clouds.

"Ge' back, boy," Zach growled at the animal and, as it moved off, he forced himself into a sitting position, feeling for any broken bones. Inquisitively, the horse advanced to stretch its neck nervously towards him again. "Back, damn ya, you stupid animal," he cursed, slapping its hairy muzzle.

The horse snorted. It jerked its head in alarm, and backed off further this time, allowing Zach to see the cause of the roaring. The man-made lake was disappearing fast, foaming white as it surged relentlessly past him, spewing through the opening Lo Ming had created with the dynamite. Fascinated, he sat up to watch the relentless torrent as it dragged away more of the loosened rocks and earth, then tumbled them along as though they were made of wood, widening the gap.

"So ya made it, Sheriff."

"Seems that way," Zach was pleased to say to his clay-daubed deputy who bent over and offered a hand to help him to his feet. "An' I'm real glad you made it, son." He explored the rest of himself for damage. Apart from that wound on his head, now grown to a lump the size of a hen's egg, some bruises and a couple of insignificant cuts, he was all right. "I don't remember much," he went on, accepting the younger man's help. "When that big bang came, I guess it put me out of action for a while."

Ray's strong hand pulled on Zach's

wrist and helped the sheriff to his feet.

"Same here," the deputy explained. "One minute we was runnin' fast as bats out o' hell . . . then the next moment I was flyin' like one." He shook his head and then grinned, his teeth gleaming white in the moonlight. "Hadn't any idea at all what happened to you."

"What about Lo Ming . . . have ya seen him?"

The gleam of Ray's teeth vanished. When he answered there was some concern in his tone.

"No, Sheriff, I ain't seen anyone till I laid eyes on you. To tell the truth, I honestly believed I was the only survivor."

From behind them and further up the bank, a horse whinnied. They turned, and saw the buggy had been overturned by the blast. Lying on its side between the shafts, the horse, with its legs tangled in the traces and reins, thrashed and struggled wildly to free itself.

"G'me a hand," Zach ordered. Together they released the frightened animal before righting the vehicle. "Well the horse ain't harmed and the buggy's not too bad, so it could've been worse."

"Cloudin' over again," Ray commented. "Might have t' wait for daybreak before we can look for Lo Ming."

"We ain't waitin'," the sheriff stated blandly. "The little fella could be out there dyin' for need of help. No son, we're gonna search for him, and now!" With that he unclipped one of the oil lamps from the buggy and passed it over to the deputy. "Put a match to the wick in that, and I'll use the other one. We'll find that little guy, supposin' we have to move every rock, twig or blade of grass in the territory."

"Don't think the little fella made it, Sheriff," Ray said quietly. "We were real lucky to get away with it, but him . . . he couldn't have stood a chance. Hecky-me, he was way behind us, still down the slope. He's gotta be dead."

"Lo Ming?" Zach shook his head determinedly. "He ain't dead. I just know he ain't. Don't ask me how I know that. I just do. There's no way I'll ever accept anythin' different . . . unless we find 'im, and I can see with my own eyes."

It had been daylight for more than an hour when, depressed and tired, Zach and Ray turned to trudge back along the bank to head upstream once more. All night long they had searched diligently along the water's edge for more than two miles but had found nobody, not even anyone belonging to the Double D bunch.

By the time, they approached where the dam had been, the water in the creek had returned to its normal level. There was no longer a cascading roar of white water, only the same gentle flow that Zach had seen on his first entry into the valley.

"Seems you were right after all," he admitted with a shoulder-heaving sigh. "Losin' that little Chinaman's like . . . " He paused and swallowed once or twice to gain time enough to compose himself before going on "Yeah . . . like losin' my only brother."

Ray grimaced and, unable to offer much comfort, gazed down at his feet in his embarrassment.

"What's that?" Zach stopped walking. Shielding his eyes with his palm he looked around. A pair of hawks were diving and wheeling in their mating ritual above the cliff tops.

"Only birds," Ray answered then walked on.

"No . . . listen!"

Both men came to a halt, holding their breath and cocking anxious ears for a while until Zach's face lit up with renewed hope.

"There," he exclaimed. "Now don't you go tellin' me that's some sort of squawkin' bird, 'cos it ain't."

"I didn't hear nothin'," the deputy stated adamantly.

"You deaf, boy?" the sheriff snapped. "Listen. There it is again."

119

"Uh-huh. You're right. Somebody's callin' . . . up there." Ray's arm, extended as straight as an arrow, pointed at the cliff face close by, and on their side of the creek where the dam had been. "But that don't say it's him."

"Think I don't have the gumption t' know that? Come on, it could be him," yelled Zach over his shoulder. "Anyhow, we gotta try." Hope rekindled within him as he began to scramble up the still-wet and slippery bank. "Quick. This ain't the time for lingerin'." Then raising his voice he shouted out, "Hold on . . . we're comin'."

"Supposin' it's not him. What happens if it's one of the Double D riders?" Ray argued.

"We'll have to cross that bridge if and when we come to it." Zach's words were hard, but inside he knew he would never harm an already injured man . . . no matter who he was.

Drawing closer to the cliff face and the spot where Ray had first indicated, the lawmen stopped in their tracks as a small quantity of soil and loose stones suddenly trickled and tumbled down towards them. The debris came from the side of a huge sloping slab of rock which jutted out from the cliff. The sheriff cupped his hands to form a megaphone around his mouth and then took a deep breath.

"Hello!" he boomed out loud and long. "Anyone there?" Together they waited, anxiously listening for any reply.

A muffled but recognizable shout rewarded them.

"Boss! . . . it me . . . Lo Ming."

★ ★ ★

By the time Lo Ming had lit the last of the fuses, he had realized there would be insufficient time for him to follow his companions. So, he did what he considered to be the next best thing. Instead of making for the horses on the other side of the dam, he ran sideways to seek shelter under the cliff by the side of the dam. The backshooters from the Double D had seen him and had given chase, hoping no doubt to capture him for a hostage, a bargaining pawn, in their game.

Pursuing the Chinese deputy had proved to be their undoing. Just as Lo Ming had reached what he thought to be the comparative safety of a shallow cave, the dynamite had exploded, sending the would-be assassins screaming to hell on a tidal wave of water and flying rocks.

The first ripple of explosions had hurled the Chinese deputy helplessly against the rear wall of the cave, half stunning him and confusing his mind. The next blast had brought down an avalanche from higher up the cliff, almost filling the cave and turning it within brief seconds into a sealed tomb.

Alone, in total darkness, and walled in like a pharaoh of ancient Egypt by tons of rock, without food or water,

Lo Ming had been tempted to give up the fight to live. His limbs had grown numb with cold and only his innate sense of duty owed to Zach had made him struggle to survive.

It had been long after sunrise when he had first seen the single glimmer of light coming in through an unsealed crack connecting him to the outside world of the living. Without tools he had clawed away at the rubble with his bare hands. Scraping at the clay, twisting and heaving, freeing individual shattered pieces of stone, he had gradually enlarged the crack until he could see the sky and feel a draft of air on his face. That had been when he had called out for the first time.

Now here he was, being dragged out from his overnight grave. The sun had climbed to its zenith. As he emerged it beat down upon him, warming his shivering limbs, and bringing him back to life. Lo Ming, bruised and battered, blinked in the brightness as he smiled at Zach.

"Thank you, Boss," he said sincerely as he bowed his head. "Thank you for saving this worthless person."

Reaching out his big hand, Zach gave the rescued man's shoulder a friendly punch, followed by a brotherly squeeze. When he spoke, his words were hardly raised above a gruff whisper.

"Glad t' help out . . . any time," he answered before reminding the Chinaman, "but don't you forget, I owed you from way back."

* * *

Arriving back in town, each sensed how different the atmosphere of the place had become, compared with how it had been when they had left. The townsfolk watched them walk their horses past them in silence, without the usual smiles and verbal greetings.

"Wonder what worm's eatin' at them?" the sheriff mentioned to his deputies riding alongside the buggy. "Looks as if someone around here's been handin' out free lemons t' suck."

He broke off and stared open-mouthed with surprise. The sheriff's office had come into view. The smooth adobe walls, which only the previous morning had been bright and whitewashed, were now cracked and smoke-blackened. Even before dismounting they could see, through the charred frame of the open doorway, tumbled heavy timbers of the collapsed roof still smoking on the remains of the office floor.

"What in the . . . ?" Zach blurted out. "Abe!" Zach's guts twisted into knots as he shouted and climbed stiffly down from the driving seat. "Where's the oldtimer . . . an' Bronco?"

"Abe's nowhere in here, Sheriff," Ray confirmed after having made a quick search of the cell block. "And neither's Bronco. His cell door's wide open."

"I've got the oldtimer at my place," someone called from the doorway.

Twisting around Zach recognized the white-aproned storekeeper.

"Oh, it's you Harry. At your place, ya say?"

"Yeah, me an' a couple o' the boys from the saloon hauled him out of here, before he burned t' death. He's been shot a couple of times, but he's game and still hangin' on to life by the skin of his teeth."

"Has a doc seen him?" Zach interrupted the mercantile owner. "And who did it? The Double D crowd?"

Harry wiped his hands needlessly on his white apron. He wasn't the type to court trouble from anyone . . . especially when he didn't know what the outcome would be.

"Doc Hankin. He dug the slugs out and since then, keeps on droppin' by to check on Abe." Pursing his lips, his fingers tugged at his moustache while he considered for a second or so before answering the next question. "Didn't see the jail-break myself . . . The whole place was on fire, burnin' like a torch

126

and past savin' by the time I got here. The whole show was over and done by then, but it was the Double D bunch all right. They rode in t' town all crowin' as perky as a Mexican fightin' cock, as though they didn't give a hoot about the law or anythin' else," he explained, waving a hand at the open doorway. "Ask around. Like I said, they made no secret of it. Plenty of folks saw them."

"Yeah, that figures, don't climb on yer high horse, I believe ya. They'd think we'd been wiped out and that they'd have a free rein in town." Anger showed in Zach's lean, sun-tanned features, and his eyes seemed to pierce into the distance. Firm lips curled back in a snarl and when he talked, his words were filled with venom. "Well we ain't wiped out and Dan Dawson's gonna discover that's a fact. Yes sir, the whole gunslingin' mob of 'em will find that out . . . and soon!"

"What exactly do we aim t' do Sheriff?" Ray Jackson butted in. "I mean, it ain't as if we're an army, and as for what you said about that telegraph message Dawson's sent . . . hell, I don't see us standin' much of a chance. When those new fellas come." He stopped, searching for the words to express his doubts without seeming to be a coward. "They're mercenaries . . . trained gunslingers. They're professionals."

Zach gazed sadly back at Ray.

"D'you get paid, son?" he asked quietly.

The deputy thought for a moment, looking for the catch he sensed was hidden in the question. Finally he answered doubtfully, "Yeah — sure I get paid."

"If you get paid for what you're doin'," Zach explained, "you're professional . . . right?"

"Well," Ray was still filled with doubt. "But . . . " he began to argue until the sheriff cut him short.

"No buts, son. We get paid to uphold the law and use guns if we have to." He turned to leave and jerked his head at the doorway. "Well, it looks as though we're gonna have to. So that's that! Savvy?"

\* \* \*

In his agony, Abe looked even older than his actual age as he lay in the bed at the back of the mercantile storeroom. His weathered skin hung grey and limp against his cheekbones and his mouth sagged open to ease his breathing. With each painful breath he sucked in, his forehead wrinkled and puckered some more in reaction to the pain.

Zach and the others could all hear the air gurgle and squeak inside his bandaged chest.

"Don't keep him talkin' for any more than a minute, Sheriff," the doctor warned in a confidential whisper. "I don't want him bustin' the stitches and haemorrhaging again. He's already lost more blood than he can spare."

129

Thinking along these lines, Zach decided on a plan to keep the stress to a minimum.

"Now Abe," he joshed, "you've got the easy part in this. I'll not keep ya long. I just want you to lie there, relax if ya can, and listen. I'm gonna ask you some questions, but there ain't no need for you to speak. All ya have t' do is blink your eyes. Once if the answer's yes . . . twice if the answer's no. And," his grin widened, "you've guessed it . . . three times straight if ya don't know. Got that?" He smiled and watched the oldtimer's eyelids. The lids closed with definite purpose, once. "Good, we're doin' real fine."

The doctor horned in to check the wounded man's pulse. Satisfied, he nodded to Zach and withdrew to the background.

"Was Dawson there with his boys?" he asked, then waited.

Abe blinked twice. "Were there any strangers with them?" The eyelids fluttered twice again. "Who shot you, was it Bronco?"

Without the slightest hesitation, the pained eye shut tight . . . once. Zach nodded his understanding and made a promise to the old man. "I'll get him for ya, Abe. Now you grab some shut-eye while you've the chance. Me an' the boys'll see to what needs to be done."

Abe attempted to smile his understanding but it was a poor effort and they left quietly, none of them sure if they would ever see the oldtimer alive again.

Lo Ming grabbed at Zach's arm and stopped him from leaving. The Chinese deputy's grin would have looked good on a Halloween pumpkin as he pointed to some new boxes stacked up neatly in the corner of the store room. A printed notice standing against them proclaimed: 'Danger No Smoking — Dynamite'.

Harry, the storekeeper, noticed and came to explain.

131

"New delivery. Arrived this mornin'. Didn't expect it. This stuff wasn't due for another month but the company sent it along with another order, to save on delivery costs I guess."

Lo Ming whispered earnestly to Zach.

"We take, Boss. Dynamite pretty good stuff. Better than black powder. Better than bullets. Yes?"

The sheriff didn't answer directly. Instead he spoke to the storekeeper. "We'll take it, Harry," he said.

Harry smiled, always pleased to do business.

"Sure, Sheriff," he enthused, rubbing his hands as usual on his apron again before taking out his order-book and licking his pencil. "How much you want?"

"All of it."

"All?" Harry gasped in his astonishment. "There's enough explosives there to fight another war."

"Funny you should say that." The sheriff grinned at his deputies. "That's

132

pretty close to what we had in mind." He turned to go again but stopped and scratched at the bristles on his chin. "While you're about it, we'll take all the detonators an' reels of fuse you can muster."

"But when d'you want it all?" Harry's hands were working overtime on his apron. "I've no help in today. It'll take time."

"You've got time. Me an' the boys are goin' to the barbers to grab us a shave an' a hot bath apiece. Afterwards, we'll be stuffin' our faces with two-pounder steaks and a couple o'cold beers across the street at Lucy's place. We'll pick the stuff up when we get back." He looked around at his deputies. "That suit you?"

"Suits me fine," Ray agreed readily, his mouth already watering.

"Whoops," Zach said. "A slight alteration — no beer for you, Ray. You can have sarsaparilla."

# 7

THE three lawmen and the storekeeper were in the yard behind the mercantile, engaged in loading the dynamite on to the buggy. Their work was almost completed when Harry's wife, flustered and in some distress, came out to the yard.

"Sheriff Scott — he's asking for you."

"Who?" Zach responded; then the woman's message sank in and his previous happy mood began to wane. Beside him, her husband and the two deputies made no comment but, sensing trouble, they stopped working to watch and listen. "Ya mean, Abe?"

"Yes, he looks bad," she admitted taking a step back towards the doorway. To hurry him, she beckoned with her crooked finger. "He's running a fever." She bit her lip and seemed to be verging

134

on tears. "I think someone should fetch the doctor."

"Ray! Go get the doc," Zach said quietly as he turned to go back through to the storeroom with the others trailing behind. "Tell him to get his fat arse over here, quick." Then he remembered the woman was present so he shrugged a little and murmured, "Sorry ma'am, I don't usually cuss in front of a lady."

Harry's wife gave him a brief, tight-lipped smile but made no mention of his slip. She had heard a lot worse than that, before her husband had saved her from spending the rest of her life in the Golden Garter in Phoenix.

Abe lay bathed in sweat, and the bandage wrapping his chest showed new blood soaking through. Pain twisted his face and each gasp of breath taken through his wide open mouth, sounded laboured and noisy. He opened his eyes as he sensed Zach's presence and raised his head from the pillow to speak.

"I'm burnin' up, Sheriff."

"Yeah, we know, Abe," Zach answered

as he drew closer, "but ya know you're not helpin' yourself any with all this gabbin'. Hell, fella, you're supposed to be restin', so do everyone a favour — lie back and wait for the doc."

Abe tried to smile.

"Jesus. Sheriff, both you an' me, we know that gettin' the sawbones out of his bed's a waste of time. As for me gabbin' . . . if I don't have my say now, I never will again." He laughed weakly as if he'd told some huge joke, but the laugh soon changed to a cough and his agony was displayed in his face.

Harry's wife took a wet rag from a bowl of cold water and wrung it out before gently dabbing and wiping the beaded perspiration from her patient's face and neck.

"What a ridiculous thing to say," she remonstrated as she worked the cloth over him. "That's a wicked thing for a Christian to even think. You ought t' be ashamed, a man of your age, jokin' like that."

Abe made another effort and winked cheekily at her.

"The sheriff an' me know all about jokes." His eye found and fixed upon Zach's. "Don't we . . . eh?" The cough started once again and the bloodstain on the bandage grew in diameter. He attempted to sit up, seeking relief by holding his wizened hand to his bubbling chest.

"Steady, oldtimer," Zach counselled as he dropped to one knee before leaning over to support the sick man with his arm. "Take it easy. We're all rootin' for ya."

Abe lay his head weakly back against the arm supporting him and, as his breathing settled, he looked up.

"When I'm gone — in case you're a-wonderin', there ain't no kin to worry about." He stared directly into Zach's unblinking eyes and asked, "Will ya do me a favour — when I've hung up my saddle?"

Zach nodded but said nothing. Instead he waited for the old man to take another couple of breaths before making his last request in full.

"Sacred promise mind ya. It's a promise to a dyin' man an' there ain't nothin' more sacred than that."

"Yeah . . . my sacred promise," Zach confirmed. "What is it?"

"Get him Sheriff." His words were spoken so low now that they sounded more like a series of hisses, and Zach had to strain his ears to hear. "Get that bastard Bronco . . . for me. Will ya do that?"

"You can take bets on it."

"Ya swear!" His eyes bulged suddenly and he gasped, one scrawny hand reaching out to claw at and grasp the front of the sheriff's shirt.

"I swear Abe. I swear."

A faint, almost imperceptible smile flitted across the wounded man's drawn features. That was the time when Zach heard the doctor and Ray behind him, coming towards the bed. They were too late. Abe coughed and the bed linen was spattered with flecks of blood

138

which widened into lighter circles. The lights of life dulled and faded for ever from his eyes. He slumped and the last breath escaped from the scrawny throat in a long rattling sigh.

Sadly, laying the oldtimer back down, Zach stepped aside to permit the medical man to go through what were now, mere formalities.

"Well, that's that. Another one who's riding days are over," the doctor said with no more emotion than if he had just taken the last cigar out of a box. He carried on closing his medical bag. "But it was no surprise to anyone was it? We all knew he didn't stand much of a chance, didn't we?"

★ ★ ★

As the purple-curtained funeral coach, drawn by arched-necked, black-plumed horses, drove back down between the older graves on the town's Boot Hill, it left behind a small group of mourners. These had gathered sad-faced, silent and thoughtful around the final resting place of Abe to pay their respects and say their last goodbyes.

The air hardly moved and was uncomfortably humid, more so than normal. The time was mid-morning of the day following the oldtimer's demise.

"That everyone here?" the preacher asked, clearly disappointed as he looked around with his one good eye at the meagre audience for his oratorical skill.

"That's the lot, Preacher-man," Zach quietly confirmed. "Old Abe didn't hold with crowds."

The storekeeper's wife sniffed audibly as, behind the black veil of her hat, she held a lace handkerchief, doused in cheap perfume, to her nose. At her side, her husband, in unison with the rest of the menfolk, respectfully bared his head, and sank a freshly shaven, razor-nicked chin on to his chest, waiting for the Bible-thumper to commence.

The black-coated, fire-and-brimstone

preacher cleared his throat, opened the book and, without the need to consult it, launched into his well-rehearsed funeral service. At first he loudly spouted hell and damnation for the poor sinner who, ready-boxed, waited in the freshly-dug grave. He paused, raising his face and arms theatrically to the sky. With a sobbing voice he switched to make a plea and extol the virtues of Abe, a man he had never known.

At intervals, forked lightning split the clouds on the horizon and peals of thunder were heard above the words. As the last mournful strains of the final hymn staggered to an end, the sky above them boiled with towering black clouds which blacked out the sun.

In the cemetery, darkness descended as if it had long passed sunset, and there was a feeling of expectancy. The storm was coming nearer. Drops of rain, big, and feeling as heavy as twenty-dollar coins, spattered down. Like wet bullets, they pierced their clothes, soaking them through to the skin.

"We're in for a genuine humdinger of a rain storm, by the look of things," Harry remarked from the corner of his mouth to Zach. "If that self-opinionated preacher-fella don't hurry, that coffin'll be floatin' to the top before that gravedigger's got time to pile on enough dirt t' cover it and hold it down."

After a curt nod from the preacher, the tobacco-chewing gravedigger hurried around with a spadeful of earth, offering it to each mourner in turn. Everyone took a handful then cast the soil into the gaping maw of the grave. As if by some divine prearranged signal, as soon as the last handful of dirt rattled on to the coffin lid, the heavens opened.

The rain came down, relentless and straight, like stair-rods. Zigzag lightning flashed all around and Zach could feel the hair on his head twitch from its effect. Then the thunder which followed came so loud and immediate, that all of those present felt the primeval fear within them.

"Amen," said the preacher quickly and, snapping the Prayer Book shut, gave a brief nod, pulled up his jacket collar then scuttled away, head down, his job done.

Knowing it would be a waste of effort running to the cover offered by the buildings in the town at the bottom of the slope, the mourners trudged resolutely on.

"Just had to rain," Harry's wife snorted testily. "For four months not a drop — and today, this. An ocean in the blink of an eye."

Zach had his own problems so made no reply as he squelched through the mud. His sodden clothing clung to him as tenaciously as a thousand feeding leeches, hampering his movements and causing more discomfort. A constant stream of water poured from his square-cut chin but he ignored this, recalling the old man he had known for such a short time. Poor old Abe, he mused.

He had had more of a launchin' than a funeral.

"Boss." Lo Ming's one word interrupted Zach's line of thought, bringing him back to the present.

"Yeah, what?"

"Look — strangers."

With his mind back on the job Zach was sheriff again. Stopping to shield his eyes from the pelting rain with his hands, automatically he let his gaze follow the Chinese deputy's pointing finger.

There, crossing the track leading up to the graveyard, on the trail out of town, a group of riders pushed on with single-minded determination. Their horses shiny in the wet, with flashing hooves, kicked up a constant spray of muddy water from the flash flood running along the road. They were a mixed bunch, all different shapes and sizes. At one extreme a diminutive figure who looked little more than a child, straddled a huge black stallion. He rode next to a giant of a man who sat astride a barrel-bellied pinto that looked too small for him. Most of the horsemen were clad in yellow slickers, but others rode along without such protection, drenched, yet showing no distress at being so. On every animal, in front of each man's knee, the butt of a carbine protruded from a leather saddle holster. But apart from the usual saddle-bags, the group carried no other baggage or stores.

"Think it's them, Sheriff?" Ray asked, wiping at his face with an open hand. "They look a real mean crowd, seen from up here."

"Well, at a guess, I'd say they'll look a damned sight uglier when ya get up real close to 'em," Zach responded with a wry grin. "And it don't look t' me like them fellas are out huntin' jack-rabbits." He started walking again. "It'll be them all right. They're men with some place already staked out an' ready for 'em. Yeah, my money says they're the hired guns Dan Dawson cabled for. They've arrived sooner

145

than I'd bargained for." For a while he plodded on in silence, thinking. "Yeah," he said again. "Now I'll have to delay things a while, an' work on a brand new plan."

"Hmm! I can tell you the plans I've got in mind, an' they don't involve me in any shootin'," Ray groaned. "Sheriff, don't ya think you've got the odds all wrong? I mean, even a blind jack-ass can see that as an army we's more than a little outnumbered."

"Uh-huh," Zach answered dead-pan. "Kinda strange that. I always figured it pretty much the same way. I realized Lo Ming an' me, we'd need some extra edge — that's why I swore you in as a deputy, to put our head-count up by half again." He put on a spurt of speed and caught up with Harry and his chuntering wife.

"You want somethin' Sheriff?" the storekeeper asked, glad of the interruption.

"Yeah . . . that dynamite. Can you keep it on my buggy in your shed for another day, or maybe two?"

"Sure. You got trouble?"

"Kinda looks that way." Zach tipped his hat to the angry woman with her drenched, mud-splattered clothes, then backed off. "Thanks a heap."

* * *

Trouble came sooner than Zach expected, that same night, after the funeral. The reluctant town mayor had arranged premises for a temporary law office next to his bank, further along Main Street. Emphasizing the word 'temporary' several times during the negotiations, the leading citizen had warned against any further shenanigans such as had happened at the previous office.

"In this town, we pay our law officers to prevent trouble — not cause it," had been his last caustic remark before leaving them to do the dirty work.

Ray Jackson had hardly nailed up the name board he had salvaged from

147

the old office, when an excited, spotty-faced youth came running over from the direction of the Silver Spur.

"Hey, Sheriff," the boy panted. "The fella at the saloon told me to high-tail it over here an' tell ya there's gonna be a shootin' any minute now."

"I ain't the sheriff, boy," Ray pointed out, carrying the claw hammer and tin of nails back in to the office.

"Ya mean, ya ain't comin'? Awe heck! I don't ever see any goin's on in this town." The disappointed youth turned to go.

"Hold your horses, I'll tell him."

"No need," Zach said, pulling on his hat with one hand as he stepped out on to the boardwalk. In his other hand he swung his twin gunbelt. "I'm a-comin'." Over his shoulder he called out. "Hold the fort, Ray. If Lo Ming arrives before I get back — send him along to the saloon. Tell him to bring his twelve-gauge."

Wide-eyed, the youth tagged on, skipping sideways like a child as

148

he looked the sheriff over with the admiration of one easily impressed.

"Why d'ya need two guns Sheriff?" he wanted to know.

"'Cos, I'm a lousy shot," Zach lied. "Now clear out of my way, boy, or I'll womp your butt good like yer momma should 'ave done." The soaking he had endured earlier that day had started off the pains in his legs again, so he wasn't in the best of moods. Striding on along the boardwalk he began to buckle on his shooting irons. "You hear me, son? Go on . . . scat!"

Even before reaching the Silver Spur, he knew it was a set-up. The piano player was thumping out a tune on the keys and the singing seemed forced, and far louder than was normal for this time of the evening. Then Zach noticed four horses, tied to the hitching rail closest to the saloon entrance. Each had an identical cavalry-style carbine, sticking out from the saddle holster. Two of the horses in particular caught his eye. They were animals he recognized from earlier on that day. One was a stallion, as black as Satan and about seventeen and a half hands high. The other, a fat little pinto, had extra long stirrup leathers hanging below its belly.

Zach ran the tip of his tongue along suddenly dry lips. He felt his pulse speed up and had to fight hard to control his breathing.

"So," he whispered. "Seems some folks are in a hurry." Common sense told him to back off, to wait until he'd organized some help, but he couldn't do that. The tin star pinned to his shirt said he was number one. It was his job.

Casually, but with all of his senses on full alert, he strolled across the muddy street and made directly for the animals at the hitching rail. He checked to see no one was watching, then slackened off the saddle girths of the four horses.

"What ya doin' that for, Sheriff?" the spotty faced youth asked from close behind him.

Zach's nerves twanged, he spun round and his right hand had almost whipped out his gun when he stopped himself.

"G'damn ya boy," he growled. "Ya could 'aye got yourself shot." He jerked his thumb hard, away from the saloon. "Now you get the hell out of here, like I said. An' keep your mouth shut!"

Once the petulant youth had gone from the scene, Zach spent a few seconds composing himself. Easing the pistols in their holsters, he flexed his fingers a couple of times then, taking a deep breath, strode up to the swing doors then stopped to look over them.

There were not many customers in the bar room. Certainly not enough to warrant all the noise that was being kicked up. Some men sat at tables, drinking, smoking and playing stud. Others sang at the top of their voices, obscene words to a popular song. Over at the long bar, a lone man leaned on one elbow as he poured whisky from the bottle in front of him.

151

In spite of the solo drinker not standing to his full height, Zach could tell he was a big man in every way: much taller than himself, and heavier too. On his head he wore an old and battered stovepipe hat from which long greasy hair stuck out from under the brim like a busted horse-hair mattress. The remainder of his clothing was modelled along the same lines — unkempt and filthy. There was however, an important exception. His gunbelt. This was immaculately cared for and the carved ivory butt of his presentation Colt was a work of art.

Although the stranger was no longer cloaked by the yellow slicker, there was no doubt in Zach's mind that before him stood the rider of the pot-bellied pinto hitched outside.

The black stallion's master was not immediately visible and the sheriff had to surmise he was sitting among the others at the tables. He felt his own guns as a kind of reassurance then breasted the doors and stepped inside.

The singing tailed off and died. The card-sharps stopped in mid-game and turned to look at him. After a few bars, the piano player realized he was on his own and, self-consciously, stopped playing too. Only one man didn't bother to turn his head. He just looked ahead into the mirror behind the bar and drank his whiskey.

Zach strolled to the end of the bar where it curled around to meet the wall. Here he could keep his eyes on what was going on, yet still be afforded a degree of protection for his back and the lower part of his body.

"Just got a report sayin' somebody was gonna get shot, in here," he stated to the abnormally nervous bartender. "Is that anywhere close to bein' right?"

The barman didn't answer right away. White-faced, he made an elaborate show of breathing on a glass, then with his cloth, continued polishing it until it squeaked. At that point, the man wearing the stovepipe hat spoke up.

"That's right lawman," he said

without turning, yet still watching through the mirror. "A fella in here's gonna get himself shot . . . any time now."

The stranger's slow and deliberate drawl was coldly delivered. Zach couldn't help but feel that same old twinge of alarm that always got him on his toes when a life-and-death fight was in the offing. Here we go again, he thought and cursed inwardly because of the pang of fear these moments always gave him. Without betraying his feelings, he answered back. "Oh, is that a fact, Mister whatever-your-name-is. And just who d'you think that's goin' t' be?"

The big man took his time in standing up to his full height. Towering above everyone else in the room, hoping to gain a psychological advantage over any opponent, he tipped his glass and drained it slowly down his throat. Smacking his lips loudly he then slapped the glass down hard on the polished mahogany bar-top.

154

"The name you're a-lookin' for, Sheriff, is Bently. Big Bill Bently. That's the name they give me on all them 'Wanted' posters you lawmen keep on nailin' up all over this state." He leered suddenly and turned to face Zach. "Maybe you've heard of me."

Zach looked puzzled. He shook his head after a pause apparently to think on the question.

"Nope," he said at last. Then he sniffed, twisting his face in disgust. "You must be small fry." Shaking his head he continued, "The smell's familiar but the name escapes me." He stared straight into the other's dirt-ingrained face. "Now about this other fella . . . the guy who's supposed to be gettin' himself filled full of bullet holes?"

"That's you, Sheriff."

The silence shattered as card players and serious drinkers gave up their pursuits and went in an immediate and quick search of personal safety. Tables were knocked aside and piles of gambling chips went rolling all over the sawdust covered floor. Panicking men tripped over upturned chairs, and spittoons were sent spinning by careless boots in the rush to evacuate the danger zone.

"Oh yeah!" Big Bill said as though just remembering something important. "Dan Dawson, he says t' tell ya g'bye an' that he hopes your dyin's gonna hurt, like you've been branded on yer pecker."

On the extreme edge of his field of vision, Zach became aware of three men still gathered around a table. They stood there, grinning.

In the other direction he was conscious of the pale-faced bartender backing slowly along to the exit flap at the far end of the bar, anxious to get clear of any spare lead that was likely to be flying around looking for a home. He reached the heavy wooden flap and raised it so that he could leave.

"Well, there ain't much point in us wastin' time gabbin' about this'n that. I'm in a mood t' do me some serious drinkin'. So Sheriff, just you get ready t' meet your Maker." He spread his legs to steady himself, put his left hand behind his back to hold his jacket clear of his pistol butt and began to stoop. "Don't think you can duck behind that bar, 'cos you ain't gonna live that long."

Zach's sinews and muscles tensed like trap springs. He saw the other man's eyes, glassy-bright in their madness. He watched the man's right shoulder dip a fraction and knew that this was the time to draw.

A loud crash came from behind Big Bill as the bartender panicked, threw caution to the wind and let the flap crash down as he made his escape to safety. For a split second the mercenary's attention was diverted, but that infinitely short time-lapse was enough. The muzzle of Zach's Colt came up above the level of the bar to blast and buck twice in rapid succession.

The first bullet shattered the half-drunk bottle of whisky and flattened itself out before tearing a hole as big as a fist high up in the ponderous belly. The second slug smashed through the already dying man's ribcage and demolished his heart. Big Bill's legs twisted together as he spun around. One arm outstretched stiffly as though seeking support as it trailed along the bar, sweeping off glasses, that then fell with him as he slumped down on to the sawdust.

Above the bar-top a lazy smoke-ring from Zach's Colt hovered and twisted. There was a period of shocked stillness then movement around the only occupied table in the bar room.

"You can hold it right there," he warned. "I want you fellas."

Immediately a hail of pistol shots came his way. Ducking down he heard tables going over as protective shields for the gunmen. The noises progressed towards the swing door and Zach guessed that the dead man's partners were keen to be on their way out . . . and fast.

Crouching low, he backed towards the barman's entry to the bar. Pushing at the half-door under the counter flap he detected a movement. One of the gang, isolated from the others, was doing the same as he was, at the other end of the bar. The man snapped off a shot and the slug splintered the woodwork close to Zach's right ear, as he in turn, with more deliberation, fired his Colt.

The target looked surprised. With his pistol arm still held in the firing position, he sagged sideways against the doorframe. An involuntary impulse caused him to jerk the trigger, his shot striking the bar mirror which clattered down on to neatly-piled drinking glasses and bottles of spirits.

The unintentional diversion allowed the others time to make a swift gun-firing exit. Zach eased himself from behind the bar in time to see the saloon doors still swinging. There were more shots fired and plenty of loud swearing outside in the street. Suddenly a twelve-gauge boomed out and he knew that Lo Ming had arrived on the job.

With the Colt still at the ready, Zach burst through the swing doors and did a crouching roll out on to the boardwalk. Out on the street there was uproar as excited and curious townsfolk were already gathering around a would-be runaway who lay face down in the mud by the hitching rail. Beside the corpse, three horses with their saddles hanging under their bellies pranced and tossed their heads in agitation.

"One man get away Boss," Lo Ming explained as he cuddled his shotgun to his chest. "Sorry."

"Hey," one of the crowd butted in. "Sheriff, I've been robbed. I saw it happen. A little guy. When the saddle on his horse slipped, he just grabbed my mare and rode off. What you gonna do about it, eh?"

Zach pointed at the black stallion.

"Ya like that?" he asked the belligerent citizen.

"Sure do, but what's that got t' do with my problem?"

"That was his animal . . . take it. I reckon it'll be a better than good trade for the one you've just lost." He noticed the wide-eyed youth who had first called him to the saloon, still hanging about. "Here boy," Zach called out, flipping him a dime. "Go tell the undertaker he's got some work waitin' for him out on the street here." Then he remembered. "Oh, and some more in the saloon, both sides of the bar."

# 8

"WHY oh why, couldn't you have arrested this poor fellow?" the town's mayor demanded to know. Pompously he pushed through the morbid bystanders and looked down with disgust at the corpse. "I'm beginning to think the original problem's no worse than the potential cure." Red-faced and conscious of the closeness of the next election, he then seized upon the chance to display his authority to the voters. "Sheriff," he went on severely, "do you always have to use the brute force of firearms and the killing that goes with them, to do your job?"

The onlookers sensed a clash of personalities, a showdown of sorts. As one man, they moved in closer, to listen and watch for the sheriff's reaction. Unperturbed, Zach took little notice of them. Instead he stared coldly at the public official.

"No, we could leave off our gunbelts . . . paint a target on our shirts, then wait around for the hoodlums t' fill us with lead. And then we'd do all the dyin'. But I don't think that would solve your problem, would it?" Zach bent down and released his holster ties to ease his leg before carrying on in the same dour manner. "On the other hand, you're forgettin', this town don't have a jail any more. Maybe you'll tell me this: if me or a deputy takes a prisoner . . . where we gonna keep 'em?" He raised his eyebrows in an expressive but mock question. "Your place, maybe?" With a smile and a wave of his arm he indicated the onlookers. "Or maybe all these good law-abidin' citizens are pushin' forward to volunteer their places."

"I . . . er, I," the mayor stammered. The colour drained rapidly from his cheeks as he desperately searched his mind for an answer. He cast an eye at the crowding voters, who then stopped their crushing advance. Instead, they pushed back again, to leave him clearly standing alone with the problem set by the sheriff.

The lawman carried on. "And another thing. I've only two deputies left. I can't afford to waste the time of any one of 'em to guard any no-account prisoner."

"Oh you can't, eh?" The mayor pounced, sensing an advantage. "*You* can't afford!" he boomed sarcastically. "Listen t' me, Sheriff, think back on who pays your salary."

"Ha! Ya think I'm in this for money?" Laughing loudly, Zach moved towards the sea of people. The sea parted. Like Moses, he walked through, shaking his head. "Money?" he jeered loudly for all to hear. "Mister Mayor," he called over his shoulder, "I dare say I could buy-out anyone in this town . . . for cash." Half-turning to the Chinese deputy who had kept pace alongside, he asked, "Well, is that right or ain't it?"

"Sure, that true, Boss." Lo Ming turned then walked backwards, nodding seriously as he told the crowd. "It true. Can buy. He rich like he say. Sheriff not lie."

★ ★ ★

With both deputies riding alongside, Zach drove the buggy over the hump in the trail, then down, towards the adobe homestead of Josh Naylor. Apart from the layer of rapidly drying mud everywhere, the sod-buster's place didn't appear to have suffered too badly because of the flood.

Not until they entered the yard did they see the owner of the property hurry across from the corral, waving his arm and in a distraught state.

"I'm mighty glad you've dropped by, Sheriff. You're just in time, I've got trouble," the agitated nester stated before Zach had properly left the driving seat and his men had dismounted.

"Ain't we all," sighed Zach as he eased himself down and rubbed his thighs to bring back the circulation. "The same trouble as last time, or somethin' a mite different?" he asked easily, refusing to be flustered as they followed the older man up the wooden steps to the veranda.

"It's my Ellie. She's in trouble."

The sheriff twitched up an eyebrow and the deputies exchanged glances but waited saying nothing.

"No, not that. I never meant *that* sort o' trouble. You evil-minded varmints!" Josh snarled in sudden anger as he realized how the others had taken his news. "I mean, she's gone . . . been took."

"Oh. When was that?" the sheriff queried, passing from the sunlight into the warm oppressive gloom of the house. "And how d'ya know that?"

"She'd only been away for maybe half an hour, Sheriff," Josh Naylor

166

explained. "She was out checkin' the fences, t' see they ain't been cut again." For a second or so he paused, swallowed once or twice then inhaled deeply before carrying on. "The next thing I knowed, her horse came gallopin' back into the yard on its ownsome and all lathered up like a whiskered chin in a barber's chair." Clearly on edge, he shoved his fingers through the remains of his hair.

"An' ya think she's lyin' out there, hurt maybe, with a broken leg or somethin'?" Ray broke in.

"Well, that's along the lines my mind went at first. I thought she must've had an accident — a fall or somethin' like that. But I should've knowed better. Ellie can ride like she was born in the saddle. She'd never be fool enough to take a risk that would cause a tumble."

"But it happens, even to the best of us, and your daughter's no exception t' that," Zach pointed out. "What makes

167

you so sure she's been took against her will?"

The nester fingered inside his shirt pocket and with a flourish produced a crumpled sheet of paper with a message on it, written in ink.

"This! This is what makes me so damned sure." As Zach took it to read, Josh told him. "That was shoved under her horse's saddle girth." Banging the table with his fist he swore. "G'damn that Dawson fella. I never thought even he'd sink so low."

"Dawson?" Ray cut in again. "Why that fella's so darned low down, he could dance under a rattlesnake and still keep his high hat on."

After studying the wording of the note carefully, Zach folded the paper before slipping it safely away into his own vest pocket.

"Well, you're right, Josh," he agreed thoughtfully. "They've taken Ellie . . . and it wasn't a spur of the moment job either."

"How d'ya know that, Sheriff, about

it not bein' spur of the moment?" Ray asked, failing to conceal the doubt in his own voice.

"That's an easy one to answer, ain't it Lo Ming?" Zach grinned, detecting a hint of a smile twitch the Chinaman's cheeks. "Go on, you tell him."

"You see note?" Lo Ming raised his eyebrows to the perplexed face of his fellow deputy.

"Uh-huh . . . as much as you did. So what?" Ray felt at a sudden disadvantage, being questioned in this way. "How'd you know somethin' I don't, eh?"

"You have eyes to see with." Lo Ming canted his head to one side in his normal manner. "Me also . . . yes?"

"Yeah, I guess so. Go on." Ray began to look doubtful, like an already beaten man. "Out with it."

"Message written on paper . . . yes?"

"Uh-huh."

"How words written . . . pencil?"

Both the sheriff and his Chinese deputy watched the third lawman's features alter as the meaning sank in to his mind. Suddenly he grinned broadly and made a helpless gesture with his hands.

"Snakes alive, fellas." Ray struck his forehead with the flat of his hand. "You must think I'm real dumb," he told them. "It's so simple a blind old mule could see it. That note, it had to be written where a pen and ink was real handy . . . an' nobody ridin' a horse would have that kinda stuff wih 'em, would they, eh?"

"And so?" prompted Zach.

"Whoever wrote it, was likely at the ranch or some such place. And, if Ellie had only been gone for half an hour before her horse came home . . . there wasn't time to take her back to the ranch, write the note then give the horse a whack on its rump for the animal to get back here so soon. Grinning smugly now, Ray explained further. "The note had to be written well in advance . . . so it was planned."

"Never mind the whys an' wherefores," the nester barked out. "How about some action from you fellas? You've been mouthin' off for nigh on five minutes when ya should've been ridin' hell for leather to the Double D."

"Just like that!" Zach remarked back at him. "What d'ya expect me to do with only two men . . . surround the whole bunch at the Double D, flash my badge then arrest 'em all?"

Josh looked as though he was going to snap back an answer, then he stopped himself and thought for a while. Then he spoke in a more subdued voice.

"Well, somethin's got to be done." He crossed the room and stood gazing at a faded sepia photograph of his wife, that hung drying on the still damp wall. "My Ellie . . . she's all I've got." Dejectedly, he turned to look at the sheriff. "If you can't get her back safe . . . well, I can't just leave her in the hands of men such as them."

"We'll get her back, mister," Ray Jackson told the distraught nester confidently. "Won't we Sheriff?"

"Well if you don't do it quick, I ain't gonna hang around waitin'. This land ain't worth a fart in a windstorm, not without my Ellie. I'll sign this place over, lock, stock and barrel to Dawson and clear out like it says in that note."

"Listen," Zach began quietly, "I've a whole load of explosives outside on my rig. We were on our way to settle up with Dawson's mob when we stopped by here. I'd everything planned." He stopped, flapped his arms helplessly then, with a heavy sigh continued, "But that's all changed, now that they're holdin' Ellie. Dawson's spiked our guns. We can't take the risk of usin' dynamite . . . and that was gonna be the ace up our sleeve. Our heavy artillery, so t' speak."

\* \* \*

For hours Ellie, trussed up like a Thanksgiving turkey, with a sweat-soaked bandanna wrapped and tied tightly around her mouth, had felt humiliated and as angry as a bear with toothache. Unceremoniously slung like a sack of flour across the front of the Mexican's ornate saddle, she was helpless. Behind her back, rawhide bindings bit into her wrists, numbing her hands as Manuel's clawing fingers held her still.

Head hanging down, her hair fell like a screen over her face each time she raised it, curtaining off her view of the passing scenery. At first she had assumed they were taking her to the ranch-house of the Double D, but after a while she knew they had travelled too far to be going there. The flat ground of the prairie had changed into rougher hill country and the horses had to work harder as the steepness increased. Soon her face was lathered by the white foaming flecks of sweat from the horse which carried her and the sun was scorching her back where her shirt had slipped out of her blue jeans.

"Better watch out for ya pecker with that little hell-cat," she heard one of her captors shout from a nearby horse. "She came close to bitin' my thumb in two. Reckon she would've too, if I hadn't punched her in the ear."

Ellie remembered the uncouth owner of the voice and could picture him in her mind's eye. He was one of the gang of mercenaries that Dawson had sent for. Then the man with whom she shared a horse, answered boastfully, "You gringos, you know not'ing about making love. You don't know how an *hombre* should handle a woman."

If Ellie had not been so tightly gagged, she would have screamed out aloud. Without warning she felt the hot stinging slaps of the Mexican's hard-skinned hand hurt her backside several times, then cruel fingers reached down to grip the back of her neck with painful bruising pressure. Then, laughing he shook her head until her teeth rattled.

"That, *hombre*," he boasted when

he had finished and released the grip on her neck again, 'ees how a man tames a woman who has fire in her veins. A man has to be rough, inflict pain, show he is the master. It is the only way. A woman needs pain. She is built for it." He heaved a romantic sigh and grinned as he explained further. "A real woman understands pain. Oh *si*, they appreciate that. In my country across the Rio Grande it is well known. Even leetle children, know that a rough man makes a good lover. *Si* . . . do not laugh *señor*, I say that is the truth."

The hand descended sharply once again on her already hotly-stinging butt.

"Thees pretty one, she is wild and strong, like a mountain cat, but she will eat out of my hand and beg me to take her to my bed . . . you see. I promise."

"Oh yeah," the one with the rag-wrapped thumb answered. "Ya mean, eat *off* your hand an' then she'll eat ya arm an' ya leg." Unable to restrain himself any longer, he laughed and others followed suit as the Mexican kicked his spiked rowels into his tired steed, sending it scrambling in jerky strides uphill, scattering the broken scree underfoot.

\* \* \*

In spite of his wounds from the barbed wire still not being fully healed, Josh Naylor had insisted upon accompanying the sheriff and his two deputies. The only concession he had made was to leave his horse behind and ride in the buggy alongside Zach.

"Take fair warnin' now, Sheriff," the nester announced as they set off, "if they've harmed a hair on my gal's head . . . well, there'll be murder done an' I don't give a tinker's cuss what happens t'me."

For ten minutes they had moved along the left bank of the creek, going downstream. Lo Ming and Ray had taken the point and rode head-down inspecting the trail.

"There!" Lo Ming slipped quickly from the saddle to kneel down and study the ground. "Three, four, five horses," he explained as the buggy drew up alongside him. "Ellie's horse go back from here, others go that way."

"That ain't the way t' the ranch-house," Ray corrected. "You've got it wrong."

"Not wrong." The Chinese deputy stood and pointed with a definite firmness of purpose. "Riders go that way."

The nester piped up. "Ya could be right at that, boy." He twisted in his seat to speak to Zach. "Them varmints, they aim t' be takin' her out to one of the line cabins. The one on the north boundary. It's set back in the cool in the shade of a stand of pines. Used to be the Three Hills relay station before the old stage line went flat broke durin' the Indian troubles."

"If that's the place," Zach broke in,

"we could be in luck . . . providin' we can get in close enough to take her guards by surprise. How far out is it?"

Josh twisted his face and scratched hard at the back of his neck as he mentally calculated the distance before he ventured to answer.

"Half a day, maybe a mite less if a fella rides hard enough."

"That far huh?" Zach mused. "Well, at least that means they'll not be able to send reinforcements to them from the ranch. Uh-huh, the way I see it, Dawson's made a big mistake. I'll bet he's got his men all staked out, ready and waitin' for us to hit his ranch from this direction . . . an' we ain't gonna oblige him." His steel hard eyes lit up as he kicked off the brake and flapped the reins. "He doesn't know it yet, but this time we're gonna put an end to Dawson's scheme once an' for all."

\* \* \*

Miserable and bruised, lying on her side where she had been dumped on the floor like a side of beef, Ellie looked around her. The place was built like a fort, out of heavy rough-cut logs and thick adobe. On every side she noticed shuttered gun ports, meant for fighting off redskins on the warpath or anyone else fool enough to attack. To her mind, it would take an army, armed at the very least with cannon, to make any impression on the defenders of such a well-constructed sanctuary. But there would be no army or cannons either, to rescue her from her likely fate. And as she recalled the Mexican's boasting, there was already a shrewd idea in her mind what that would be.

The clinking of spurs and the sound of heavy footsteps approached the doorway. She shut her eyes, pretending to be asleep but it didn't help any. A boot kicked her in the ribs.

"Hey, woman," the Mexican said as he knelt down and slashed at her bonds with his bone-handled knife.

"Food . . . the men want food. You cook, now!"

"Go to hell, you dirty greaser," Ellie began as soon as the gag was pulled down from her mouth. But she wished she had kept quiet.

The hand which had slapped her backside so hard when she had been slung across the horse, lashed out like a whip. Her cheek stung like a scald, and there was a ringing in her ears as involuntary tears streamed from her eyes. Her hair was grasped and she felt herself hauled to her feet and smelled the chilli on his breath as the Mexican held her face close to his own.

"You not shout at Manuel," he told her through clenched teeth. "You not speak to Manuel until I say . . . *si?*" When she did not give an immediate response he shook her by her hair and asked again. *Si . . . comprende?*"

"Yes . . . *si*," she had to agree.

He smiled with satisfaction.

"*Buenos,*" he told her. "You do

180

good t'ings, make Manuel happy . . . or
. . . this." He flashed his knife in front
of her eyes and holding the razor-
sharp point close to her face traced
an imaginary line across it. "Manuel,
he put his mark on you." Releasing
her hair he slipped his blade back in
its sheath then pointed through the
doorway he had entered by. "Kitchen.
Cook!"

* * *

"If I remember rightly," Josh Naylor
told Zach as he drove the buggy steadily
up a slope. "We should be able to see
the relay station once we're over the
brow of this here hill and through some
standin' timber."

"Well I ain't sorry t' hear that news,"
Zach remarked as he eased himself on
the driving seat. "My arse feels like
it'll stay flat an' sore for the rest of
my natural." He called to the mounted
deputies. "Better ride on ahead. Keep
your eyes open, boys. Josh thinks it's

just a little way over the top of this rise. You never know, they could have a lookout posted. If ya see anythin' come back an' let me know."

★ ★ ★

"Yep, it's them all right," Zach confirmed quietly after they'd hidden the buggy and the horses in the trees then moved forward on foot. "I recognize a couple o' them broncs from the day of old Abe's funeral. They belong to the new lot of gunslingers that rode in."

"An' that," the nester broke in, "the one nearest to the post beside the gate, that belongs to the Mexican, the mean bastard who enjoyed himself wrappin' me in that barbed wire." Subconsciously his hand went up to finger at the cuts which were still not fully healed on his face. "I owe that fella," he declared bitterly. "Yeah, I owe him plenty."

"Right," Zach stated emphatically,

no longer listening to the dirt-farmer. "Lo Ming, you have a scout around at the back of the place. Find out what you can about numbers an' such, but be careful." Giving the Chinaman a wink, he added, "I don't want to walk behind another man up to Boot Hill, not with the pains these legs give me."

"Well, what d' we do?" Josh wanted to know once the deputies had been despatched on their separate mission.

"Nothin', and I mean nothin' . . . unless you care to grab some shut-eye. Which when ya think on it ain't such a bad idea, considerin' we could end up havin' a heavy night." With that he sat with his back snuggled against a convenient tree, tipped his hat over his eyes, folded his arms and fell asleep.

★ ★ ★

Manuel's chair scraped noisily as he pushed it back from the table. For

183

some time he sat picking his teeth with a match as he eyed Ellie clearing the dishes.

"Got the hots real bad for that little gal, ain't ya, Mex?" Pete Ackerman, the man with the bitten thumb scoffed from his seat at the opposite end of the table.

Ellie heard but said nothing, instead she hurried her work and carried the overladen tray out to the kitchen.

Manuel stopped picking at his teeth and flicked the matchstick derisively in the direction of Ackerman.

The others around the table tensed. This was fighting talk. Prudently they pushed their own chairs back and prepared to move in a hurry, not wanting any part in the senseless argument.

"Don't call me Mex . . . the name is Manuel. Use it with proper respect, or . . . " He sneered, took out his knife and nonchalantly began to scrape out his fingernail with the point.

"Or what?" Ackerman prodded.

184

"Or," — Manuel's head was still chin down but he let his sombre brown eyes lift until they stared the length of the table into the man he had challenged — "I shut your fat gringo mouth . . . for ever."

"Hey fellas," one of the more reasonable men exclaimed. "Come on, lighten up. There ain't nothin' that's been said worth dyin' for."

"You shut up, Carter," Ackerman answered. "Keep your nose from where it don't belong . . . right?"

"Only tryin' t' help, that's all," Carter muttered. Leaving his chair and, along with the others, he stepped back to give the pair some fighting space.

The two combatants stood up at the same time, kicking their chairs aside before moving out away from the table, to where the floor was clear of obstructions.

"You dagos think yer pretty good with knives, don't yer? Well you greasers don't hold a candle to us Mississippi river boys." With a metallic click, an eight-inch blade of well-honed, polished steel flashed into view. Ackerman grinned and beckoned the Mexican to come closer. At the same time he crouched, holding his knife before him as he circled Manuel like a wolf. "Come on, greaser . . . or do you want to make this interestin', huh?"

Manuel adopted the same stance and held his own blade in a similar way to his opponent. With unblinking eyes he focused intently upon the other man's blade.

"Interesting . . . what's this you speak about, eh . . . gringo?"

Keenly alert, Ackerman continued to circle in time with the other. Speaking as casually as if he was sitting in a barber's chair, he went on to explain.

"The girl, back there in the kitchen, you want her, don't ya?"

"What of it, big mouth?"

Ackerman ignored the taunt, knowing that a man who loses his cool in a knife fight is likely to lose his life.

"You an' me. We'll have a side bet."

After a few tentative thrusts and parries to test each other's reactions, he spoke once again. "The first to draw blood gets to hump the gal and the other holds off . . . An' after that, the fight goes on . . . till the end."

Following a murmur of approval from the watchers the Mexican smiled.

"*Señor!*" He seemed impressed. "Such an idea is worthy of a poet from my own country. I applaud you for it." He held up his hand, stepped back and stood tall again, motioning the white man to call a truce. From the smile-twisted corner of his mouth he snapped an order. "Somebody, go fetch the lucky lady. Now!" Confidently he spoke across the space to the other gladiator. "Gringo, you better make your peace with God then prepare yourself to lose blood. I feel randy like a stallion. But don't worry, while you bleed I let you watch how a

Mexican *caballero* conquers a wench and makes love." His eyes crinkled at the corners and a warm, friendly smile split his face. "Then I kill you dead . . . *si?*"

# 9

TRUE to his nature, Lo Ming took his time as he sidled along with his back pressed flat against the rear wall. His senses were as taut as a harp's strings, tuned to detect and respond to the slightest sign of danger. Clasped in his delicate hands the twelve-gauge had both hammers drawn back and ready to deal out death if the need arose.

From where he was, he could see Ray Jackson with his pistol drawn. For a few awkward moments he watched his fellow deputy make his way across almost bare open ground, bellying along, diagonally like a sidewinder. Only when he had stood up after reaching the stables at the other side of the main building, did Lo Ming relax a little.

Ray turned and, with a roguish grin,

gave him the OK signal. Then he waited for a sign of acknowledgement before disappearing through the open doorway to carry out his allotted task.

The Chinaman reached one of the gunports, finding it shuttered and nailed closed. However, upon closer inspection, he saw the sun-dried wood had twisted then shrunk and split, leaving an adequate gap for him to peer through. As ever, ruled by a more than usual amount of common sense, he was acutely conscious of the sun behind him. Because of this he moved exceedingly slowly, lest his shadow showed through the cracked timber to betray his presence to an enemy inside.

At first he saw little. As he pressed his face against the crack, he shielded his eyes with one hand until they had adjusted to the difference in light levels. He was standing outside a disused store-room. Cobwebs covered everything, while a thick layer of dust promised to build up to what looked like a desert in a long hot summer, but without as much life.

He moved position slightly and was at once rewarded by the sight of a half-open door. Beyond this he could just see into another, lighter and much more spacious room. Noisy, laughing men sat around a table and appeared to be eating an evening meal. Now and again, he was pleased to catch fleeting glimpses of Ellie as she carried trays of vittles to serve those at the table.

Determined to get a better view, and add to his report for Zach, the Chinese deputy moved on. At the corner he stopped as muffled voices came to him on a slight breeze. This breeze also carried a penetrating smell which told its own story. Lo Ming doffed his hat before venturing to glimpse around the corner with one eye exposed only.

He had been right. Before him the relay station privy door hung open wide. Inside two of the gang with elbows resting on their knees, sat with their pants crumpled around their ankles.

Smoking and passing the time of day, they shared not only a two-hole plank but an aggravating squadron of buzzing flies. Lo Ming watched as one of the sitters deliberately pursed his lips, and took aim. When he spat, a fly was fixed on the doorpost for ever as though set in amber.

The Chinaman fingered the trigger of his shotgun. It would be, he mused, so easy to reduce the opposition by two, but he knew that wasn't the task he had in hand. The important things had to come first. it was information that was needed not scalps.

"Ya know somethin', Henry?" the fly exterminator voiced in a nasal whine, interrupting Lo Ming's chain of thought. The speaker paused and picked thoughtfully at his nose for a while.

"Know what?" his partner asked, unable to endure the torment of waiting any longer. "Could be . . . I know lots o' things."

"Ackerman . . . He's gunnin' for that

grease-ball Mex." He broke off for a spell, wafting his hat in front of his face and twisting his lips in disgust. "Snakes alive, Henry . . . just what in the hell've you been eatin'? You've got this privy stinkin' like a pig-keeper's workin' boots."

If Henry heard the remarks he didn't comment. Instead, he concentrated his mind on the feud between the Mississippi man and the Mexican.

"It ain't no secret. Everyone knows he hates dagos . . . 'specially the greaser. Funny that. Ackerman never did take kindly to any Mex as long as I've knowed him. Surely ya recall the job we did a year back for the railway company? The Pecos River job? Remember how he crucified them two on the boundary between the two ranches and sent the owners a note sayin' that's what would happen to their daughters." He laughed. "Frightened the shit out of 'em. The yella bastards signed away their land-rights the same day."

"Yeah, but those two he crucified, well, in my book they don't count as Mexicans . . . not real honest t' God ones. They were women, for Christ's sake. Hell, women don't count any-damned-where, now do they, huh?"

Lo Ming pulled back a little from the corner as Henry frowned and stood up slowly, his eyes gazing into the nothingness. Henry looked totally confounded by this new argument. He frowned harder, making his eyes squint with the effort as he buttoned up the flapping trapdoor of his grubby long johns. At last, as he slowly stooped to drag up his hole-riddled denim pants.

"Women or not," he argued, "the newspapers said they was Mexican." He gave a superior grin. "An' hell, fella, ain't it a fact, everybody knows, if it's in the newspaper, then it's gospel truth, ain't it, eh . . . ain't it?"

"Bullshit! Next time you'll be tellin' me yer momma's still a virgin."

Lo Ming listened in awe and once again, wondered if he would ever

194

understand Americans. With a sigh of resignation he waited patiently until finally the arguing mercenaries left the fly-besieged privy and went indoors. Then, holding his breath, Lo Ming pushed on past the odious outbuilding as quickly as he dared, before moving on to locate the next available gunport to look through.

★ ★ ★

Zach collected the various items of intelligence from his deputies after they had returned safely from their scouting missions. In spite of the sod-buster's constant urging to *do something pronto* the sheriff was taking plenty of time to make his plans. Only when he had, to the best of his knowledge, covered every eventuality, did he decide it was time to make his move. Quietly and methodically he explained everything down to the last detail; then, only when he was completely satisfied his words had been taken in, he set to and deployed his men.

"An' you grab yer gun and come along with me Josh. You ain't on the pay-roll and I feel kind of responsible for you stayin' alive." Zach grinned. "Besides, if anythin' happened to you, I don't want Ellie shootin' my hide full of holes."

"Hey, I might have a few years lead on you an' the boys, but don't let that concern you. There ain't no need Sheriff, I got clean through the war from beginnin' t' end without anyone havin' to wet-nurse me." Josh brandished his gun. "And don't you worry none about this, either. I can handle it as good as the next man."

"Glad t' hear it," Zach remarked laconically. "Come on, move your arse, we've got to work our way around that ridge and move in to be ready, before the boys do their stuff."

Within a few minutes Zach and the nester were safely behind a well-stocked log pile. It was a good position, well within sight and range of the front of the relay station's living-quarters, and enabling them to cover the whole of the yard.

"Well, Josh, that's the first part of the plan carried out," Zach said as he carefully moved some logs, rearranging them so that he could aim his guns between them. "Now if you're a prayin' man, you'd better get on to the Top-hand and put in a good word for me. Ask 'im to make me be right about plan number two."

* * *

Ellie struggled, scratched, bit and clawed at the laughing mercenaries as they dragged her to the centre of the room between the two knife fighters.

"Take your slimy paws off me," she panted with the robust effort of her exertions. "You ain't nothin' but animals. No . . . you're lower than that . . . you're scum."

The onlookers laughed and urged on

197

the ones who were doing their best to restrain her. After an otherwise dull and routine type of day, they were enjoying the welcome change her presence promised to give them.

"Call yourselves men?" She sneered in disgust at the mere idea. "There ain't one o' ya I'd let clean out my poppa's hogs. I'd have too much respect for the hogs." Suddenly, she heaved her knee up under the crotch of one of the men holding her arms.

"Oooh . . . sweet Jesus," he gasped. His eyes widened then bulged as, with both hands clawing at his crotch, he crumpled in a heap on the floor as though he'd been poleaxed. In a whispered croak he added, "I'll swing for that bitch."

Ellie managed to break away from the other captor but was pounced on before she reached halfway to the door. When she was half carried, half dragged back to the centre, Pete Ackerman was laughing.

"I'm gonna enjoy teachin' you

manners, gal," he smirked, gripping her jaw painfully between finger and thumb. "You're gonna rue the day you ever tried t' bite me, woman."

"Do not listen, *señorita*," Manuel broke in. "That man will never harm you. I will kill him for you." As her eyes turned towards him, he flashed his widest smile. "Then my leetle dove . . . we make beautiful love in my bed."

"Huh! Like hell you will," Ackerman retorted. "Let's get on with things, but first, let's all have a better look at what pleasures we're fightin' for." He stared at the Mexican. "All right . . . greaser?"

"*Si*, sure." He nodded to the men holding Ellie. "Let's see what I'm gonna sleep with." He snapped his fingers. "Strip her, fellas."

As the first eager hand clutched at her shirt and the buttons began to pop, Ellie screamed, but her cry was never noticed. The whole structure of the building shook as the blast from an explosion burst open the door and shutters of the gunports. The room filled with clouds of choking dust and an unbelievable stench which had everyone gagging and gasping for fresh air.

The fight temporarily forgotten, Manuel crossed himself as his rapidly moving lips gabbled a prayer in his native tongue.

"What in tarnation . . . was that?" Ackerman exclaimed. "Everyone grab a gun an' get to a defence position. See who did that." He pointed to the floor about where Ellie was standing. "You . . . lay down there an' don't even twitch ya nose, or so help me, I'll shoot you so full o' holes they'll use you t' strain cabbage."

Sensibly for once, she did as she was told. Lying there among the dust and spittle, a hand was clamped over her nose and mouth while her hopes rose as she listened for any clue as to what was happening outside.

"See anybody?" Henry asked.

"Nope . . . Jesus, what a stink!"

"Kinda gets t' ya, don't it?"

"Think I'd sooner be shot than stay in here."

"Me too."

The dust cloud subsided.

"Hey, you guys. The thunder-box . . . it's gone!" one of the gunmen blurted out in disbelief.

"Gone?" Ackerman repeated, puzzled.

"Sure. See for yoursel' if ya don't believe me. I can hardly believe it myself. Imagine, blowin' itself sky high." Thoughtfully he added. "I tell yer one thing. I ain't ever gonna smoke inside a privvy again."

★ ★ ★

"I sure wish Lo Ming had picked a sweeter smellin' target," Zach complained as he tied his neckerchief over his mouth and nose. "Especially when there ain't much movement of air to get rid of that stench."

"Come on, come on," Josh whispered, staring towards the main building.

"Come out, you bastards, an' get what's due."

"Be patient, and don't go lettin' off that gun too soon," Zach cautioned. "We've got to give 'em time. Let 'em all feel safe enough to come out and investigate. They're suspicious, and so would I be if I was standin' in their shoes. After all, it ain't every day that a log-built privy takes t' explodin' all over the place. It takes some understandin', don't it?"

"Somebody's openin' the door," Josh Naylor whispered, nudging Zach in the ribs with his elbow.

"Yeah, I see him."

Together they lay behind the log pile watching the figure emerge into the growing dusk of evening. Pistol at the ready, taking one step at a time, he looked all around, ready to hit the ground and fire at the slightest provocation.

"Cautious type of fella," the nester pointed out. "Not what you'd call trustin'."

"Don't blame a guy for wantin' t' stay alive," muttered Zach. "I'll bet he didn't exactly volunteer for the job. He's out there without protection, to draw fire, half expectin' every breath he takes to be his last."

"See anythin' Hank?" someone called out from a gunport.

"Nope . . . not a sign," the one called Hank answered back with obvious relief. "Come on out . . . see for yourself," he advised, wanting to share the odds on the danger.

Cautiously, one at a time, others came out, their loaded weapons waving at anything that could be deemed suspicious.

Ackerman was last to show himself in front of the doorway, but he did not step from the veranda.

"Have a good look around fellas," he warned them. "We don't want to fall for any funny stuff, do we?"

Behind the woodpile, the sheriff and the dirt-farmer waited, checking off the numbers, one by one.

"Six and the Mex," Josh counted. "He's mine."

"Same as the boys said there were," Zach pointed out. "Watch it," he warned, ducking. "That first fella's comin' our way."

As the original hesitant scout drew closer, he appeared to gain confidence with every stride, swanking even, in front of the others. By the time he reached the firewood his bravado had peaked. He stopped to roll a smoke. Not until he had lit the cigarette did his fears return, as something iron-hard and unyielding was pushed up into the crease of his backside, then held there. Behind him a whisper sounded like the voice of doom.

"Light your cigarette, son," Zach advised. "Enjoy it. Act natural, like you ain't a care in the world. And if you've a notion to make a play for your gun . . . don't. 'Cos, boy, if I decide to squeeze this trigger, you'll be wearin' your arse as a necklace."

Lo Ming had watched the last man leave by the door, and now climbed like a healthy squirrel through the open gun port of the store-room. Tiptoeing across to the door, he peeped into the main room.

"Missy Ellie!" In a flash he was kneeling by her side. To his astonishment she beamed at him, then flung her arms around his neck.

"Oh Lo Ming . . . thank the Lord."

"He ain't gonna help ya now, gal," jeered Ackerman from the doorway. He closed the door and barred it behind him, all the time levelling his Colt at the pair. "Drop that bird gun. Now . . . or I'll let you both have it in the guts."

Angry and shame-faced, the little Chinaman let the twelve-gauge slip from his hand until the butt struck the floor. Then he pushed it gently sideways to clatter on to the wooden plank.

205

"Get away from him." The Colt was jerked like a finger of death to point the way Ellie should go. "Well, chinky, chinky Chinaman, where'd you like it first?" He toyed with the pistol, changing his aim from place to place. "The belly . . . the chest, or maybe through the throat?"

"And you, you call yourself a man," Ellie spat at him. "You'd stand there and shoot a helpless, unarmed man?"

Ackerman smiled and lowered his gun.

"You're right, gal. Why waste a good bullet on a heathen chinky when I can cut his heart out with this." A flash of light reflected from the knife which he had conjured into his hand. "Come here boy." Slipping his Colt into its holster, he smiled and beckoned Lo Ming with a jerk of his head. Eyes glittering, he began his slow advance. "Old devil death's a-comin' boy."

Impassive, Lo Ming stayed where he was. Legs wide apart, knees slightly bent, he stood motionless. Slit eyes unblinking, he held his hands in front of him, slightly out and away from his body. Each fine delicate finger was lined up straight, poised as if ready to place together for prayer.

"Yeah," Ackerman smiled. "That's the idea, chinky . . . say ya heathen prayers . . . You're gonna die."

# 10

UNSADDLED horses, having been driven out by the unseen Ray, suddenly galloped from the stables to thunder among the bewildered gunhands in the yard.

"Stop 'em," Manuel screamed. "You all wanna walk back to the ranch?" The potential danger forgotten, hand-guns were holstered as they all ran to grab the flowing manes or tails of the fleeing mounts.

Within minutes the horses had been recaptured. By then laughter had taken the edge off the tension. Zach chose this as his moment. Standing up behind the waist-high log pile, his pistol still covering the cigarette smoker, he shouted for everyone to hear.

"Hold it there. All of ya . . . reach up and grab some sky. You're all under arrest. Now be smart . . . we've got ya surrounded," he warned. "We'll wipe you out if we have to."

* * *

Meanwhile, inside the relay station, Pete Ackerman lunged suddenly with an extravagant movement like a swordsman, but to his dismay discovered his knife point had stabbed nothing but air. Away to his right, Lo Ming was already adopting the same stance as before. The knife man licked his lips then grinned. "Mmm, fast on ya feet, ain't ya, little fella? Well, you slant-eyed son of a bitch, you make the most of it, 'cos you ain't gonna be movin' for much longer."

Advancing on the Chinaman with quick side to side slashing strokes, his blade searched and struck for flesh. Again finding none, dumb surprise and fear showed in Ackerman's eyes. His wrist was grasped then twisted. Numb fingers, no longer responding to his will, let the blade fall to the floor. Suddenly the Chinaman's foot became lodged under his armpit. As the oriental straightened his leg and rolled backwards, the bigger man became vaguely aware that he was flying. Fascinated, Ackerman watched helplessly as the edge of the table-top approached and the next moment struck him full in the face. When he regained consciousness, with his nose flattened and cheek-bones shattered, he would no longer be wise to boast about his good looks.

* * *

Outside, a fast gun, with more speed than brain or accuracy, drew and snapped a shot at Zach. The .45 slug flew wide, missed the sheriff and took his cigarette-smoking prisoner high in the chest. Slammed back he tumbled over the woodpile to land on and almost flatten Josh.

That single wayward shot started the

bloodshed as Zach's Colt blasted back at the fast gun, and sent him in search of the happy hunting grounds. Ducking and weaving like demented jack-rabbits in search of safety, they fired at invisible targets. Over to the right, Ray fired from inside the stable, at two other men running for cover. They crumpled then died in the dust. Bullets ricochetted in every direction, until, from a gunport, the familiar roar of Lo Ming's twelve-gauge boomed out twice. Then everything went quiet again.

Swearing angrily, Josh struggled out from under the gory corpse and loose logs. Gun at the ready, he stood up.

"It's over, Josh." Zach ejected his empty shell cases from his gun. "Relax, ya can put your gun away."

"Damn it . . . I never got a single shot off," the farmer complained bitterly as he followed the sheriff to inspect the carnage. "I feel robbed." He stopped, then moaned as he stood over the twisted cadaver of the Mexican. "That's the bastard . . . I wanted him to myself."

"Don't know why," Zach pointed out. "He's still dead. There ain't no medals bein' handed around for makin' a kill. Anyhow, that's the way it goes at times."

From the main building, Pete Ackerman, bruised and bloody, walked unsteadily ahead of a beaming Ellie who constantly jabbed him in the back with his own gun. At her side, Lo Ming grinned proudly. "Me got prisoner, Boss." Then as always, he asked, "I do good, eh?"

"Uh-huh, but do us all a favour," Zach grimaced. "Next time you use explosives, please . . . give the privy a miss."

★ ★ ★

The night had seemed to drag for ever on that long limb-cramping ride back to town with the prisoner. Dropping off a protesting Ellie at the hotel

212

for the night, they delivered the slicker-wrapped dead to the funeral parlour before seeking out the mayor to arrange with him a secure place, medical attention and a guard for Ackerman. After that, they insisted on fresh horses from the angry livery man, having dragged him in his nightshirt, cursing like a trooper on fatigues, from the warm bed of his brand-new young wife.

By the time they had rustled up a hot meal and then ridden out to the Double D, the sky in the east was showing streaks of red and yellow light on the horizon, matching their tired eyes. Plans were already laid and each of them knew the job he had been allotted. Each man was aware that the make or break battle was about to take place.

The ranch-house and outbuildings were much more exposed than had been the case at the old relay station. Here they had to leave the horses and the buggy further away, to keep

213

them out of sight of anyone standing guard duty. Because of this, the work proved to be far more arduous than they had expected. To avoid detection, the dynamite, weapons, and every other essential, had to be back-packed and carried a greater distance. Stooped over double, they at times, even had to crawl on their bellies.

"I'm bushed," admitted Ray, flopping down on his back, spread-eagled and panting as he looked up at the fading moon. "Oh boy, could I kill a bottle o'booze."

"Listen son, for a dryin' out drunk, you're doin' fine without it," Zach remarked. He sank down to sit on the yellowed grass beside him. "It's all over exceptin' the fightin' stuff . . . and the legal side." He looked to the broadening band of the cold light of dawn. "If all goes to plan, we'll be back in town before we know it."

"Sheriff," Josh's words sounded urgent. "Somethin's goin' on in the bunkhouse. A lamp's been lit."

Rolling over on to his elbow, Zach checked, decided, then said briskly, "That's it. Right fellas, time's up. Make for your positions. Let's get down to business."

"Ya reckon that throwin'-stick thing'll work?" the nester queried as Lo Ming slipped away to his place of duty. "It looks too simple to be able to do the job."

"Listen, Josh," Zach said. "If that little fella told me he could fly . . . I'd believe him." They had reached a part where they had to go down on hands and knees to crawl along a shallow dried-out gully, to keep out of view of the ranch buildings. Zach stopped to take a couple of breaths rest. "Mark my words, Lo Ming's so damned honest, it hurts. He never tells lies."

"I don't care. It's still a hell of a long way to throw a stick of explosive . . . even for a full-growed man. An' you can't tell me he's full growed."

At the point where the gully changed course, they left it. Zach led the way to a concealed spot behind the hand pump and water trough beside the corral. Here, directly opposite the house they had a good view of the deputies' battle stations as well as the bunkhouse and barn.

"So far, so good," Zach remarked gratefully as they arranged the weapons, and ammunition ready for immediate use. He tapped the water trough with his knuckle. "At least we ain't gonna thirst t' death." The early morning dew was still wet on everything. Their clothes already damp because of it, felt cold, causing them to shiver as a breeze got up.

The bunkhouse door opened. A gangling cowpoke staggered out, yawned, and stretched. Cramming his hat on his balding head, with a bow-legged gait he ambled over to the barn.

"Wonder what he's up to?" the sheriff mused out aloud.

"One of Dawson's old mob. Up an' about mighty early," Josh pointed out. "Don't look like normal routine t' me."

The sun peeped above the horizon, warming their backs and sending long black shadows towards the scene before them.

"Oh-oh that could alter things," Zach groaned, as a smart buggy and matching pair were driven out of the barn and taken up to the front of the ranch-house steps by the rangy cowboy. "Looks like someone's plannin' on taking a trip."

"I've a dollar that says it's Dawson . . . that's his custom-built rig." Josh's anger bubbled over. "Don't tell me you're gonna let him wriggle out again, Sheriff? That skunk's as slippery as an eel in a pail of hog-fat."

Zach ignored the taunt. He had his pocket watch out, counting the seconds under his breath.

"Now!" He looked over to where Lo Ming was concealed then smiled as a wisp of pale blue smoke made its arched flight through the crisp morning air, over the bunkhouse, and halfway to the barn. Three seconds later a massive explosion rent the dawn stillness like a storm.

The panicking occupants of the bunkhouse spilled out like toys emptied from a box. In various stages of undress, some had razors in their fingers, and soap-lathered chins. Others hopped as they dragged their work pants over long johns, all of them gabbling like excited turkeys.

The frantic team hitched to Dawson's driverless buggy had stampeded after the explosion. Now the terrified animals ploughed relentlessly through the stupefied ranch hands who scattered and dived aside to save their own hides.

Enjoying himself, Lo Ming kept up the dynamite bombardment until the ranch-house had been surrounded by random explosions. Zach waited until all was silent and the dust had settled.

"Hey! In the house!" he called between cupped hands. "This is the Sheriff." He hesitated while the impact of his words sank in. "I've come for two men . . . Dan Dawson and Bronco

Parks. I have warrants for their arrest."
He paused. "Anybody else who wants
to leave now, has safe passage out!"

"They'll not bite on that. Them
fellas've been around." The nester
shook his head. "They know we're
out-gunned."

"Maybe," Zach winked. "But they
ain't got dynamite."

"You'll not bluff them."

"Watch me," Zach said grimly, then
resumed shouting his message. "Don't
anyone think of tryin' any funny stuff,
not if ya wanna stay alive, 'cos
you're all surrounded." He grinned
at the head-shaking farmer next to
him. "Fellas, you've five minutes to
gather your gear and clear out. Anyone
inside after that . . . well . . . he's
gonna have t' face the music. We're
gonna blow that place t' hell an'
back."

"Bullshit, lawman." The words came
from inside the house. "We can drop
any fella who feels lucky enough to
try."

"Dawson," Josh exclaimed. "It's his voice."

As if to prove his point, the ranch owner emptied a Winchester out of a window, firing blindly through the dust cloud, his random bullets ricochetting wildly.

Following his instructions, Lo Ming lit the fuse of a bundle of three dynamite sticks, before calmly placing it in the shallow carved cup at the end of his throwing stick. He aimed at his target, drew back his arm and flicked the stick forward. With grim satisfaction he watched the tell-tale trail of fuse smoke until it entered the open doorway of the barn and disappeared into the shade.

A moment after the flash, the walls and roof of the barn seemed to swell, lift, then burst into a thousand pieces as the explosive tore it apart, scattering it like falling leaves. And, all around, wisps of hay floated in the air, drifting with the wind.

"Hold it Sheriff . . . don't shoot,

we're gettin' out . . . fast," a panic-stricken voice yelled from a broken window, downstairs in the house.

"There ain't nobody goin' nowhere." Bronco's voice was easy to recognize. A big bore revolver fired several times. The rest of the glass fell from the frame as a man flopped head down, hanging half out of the window he had called from. Behind him and out of sight, Bronco shouted again. "And that goes for anyone else who wants t' leave."

"Suit yourselves," Zach butted in at the top of his voice. "But that murderin' son of a bitch and his boss'll get ya all killed. You're all gonna end up dead if you stay inside that wooden coffin." Pausing for effect, he suggested, "Just imagine," he went on, "all blowed to little pieces . . . and for what?"

Everything happened at once. Men leaped from windows, and poured out of the front door. With weapon-free hands in the air, they ran for their lives, as Dawson, along with Bronco and a few mercenaries, shot them down from behind.

A frantic moment of indecision brought out the rancher and his foreman with some others to mount a furious attack. Staying cool, Zach selected his target, sighted, then gently squeezed the trigger. With satisfaction he saw Bronco stand, then tumble lifelessly down the veranda steps.

"That's what I promised you Abe," Zach said under his breath. "I got 'im for ya."

Three more mercenaries bit the dust, and two others were wounded. The attack fizzled out. For a while the Double D men fired from behind the supporting pillars of the veranda. Then, not liking the intense crossfire from the lawmen, they decided against running the gauntlet, and retreated to the house, leaving their dead and wounded.

Zach stopped shooting, and pulled Josh down to safety. Then he whistled, and waited, until through the air, several thin blue smoke trails, one after the other, converged on the ranch-house. In quick succession, the explosions rippled through the structure, until, when the dust had settled, all that remained was a pile of splintered lumber.

"Job's done." Zach nodded to the open-mouthed and silent nester. "Didn't I tell ya Lo Ming could do it?" He stood and waved to his deputies. "Come on fellas . . . let's go an' get breakfast."

## THE END

## FARGO: PANAMA GOLD
### John Benteen

With foreign money behind him, Buckner was going to destroy the Panama Canal before it could be completed. Fargo's job was to stop Buckner.

## FARGO:
## THE SHARPSHOOTERS
### John Benteen

The Canfield clan, thirty strong were raising hell in Texas. Fargo was tough enough to hold his own against the whole clan.

## PISTOL LAW
### Paul Evan Lehman

Lance Jones came back to Mustang for just one thing — revenge! Revenge on the people who had him thrown in jail.

# FARGO: MASSACRE RIVER
## John Benteen

The ambushers up ahead had now blocked the road. Fargo's convoy was a jumble, a perfect target for the insurgents' weapons!

# SUNDANCE: DEATH IN THE LAVA
## John Benteen

The Modoc's captured the wagon train and its cargo of gold. But now the halfbreed they called Sundance was going after it . . .

# HARSH RECKONING
## Phil Ketchum

Five years of keeping himself alive in a brutal prison had made Brand tough and careless about who he gunned down . . .

## McALLISTER ON THE COMANCHE CROSSING
### Matt Chisholm

The Comanche, McAllister owes them a life — and the trail is soaked with the blood of the men who had tried to outrun them before.

## QUICK-TRIGGER COUNTRY
### Clem Colt

Turkey Red hooked up with Curly Bill Graham's outlaw crew. But wholesale murder was out of Turk's line, so when range war flared he bucked the whole border gang alone . . .

## CAMPAIGNING
### Jim Miller

Ambushed on the Santa Fe trail, Sean Callahan is saved by two Indian strangers. But there'll be more lead and arrows flying before the band join Kit Carson against the Comanches.

## FIGHTING RAMROD
### Charles N. Heckelmann

Most men would have cut their losses, but Frazer counted the bullets in his guns and said he'd soak the range in blood before he'd give up another inch of what was his.

## LONE GUN
### Eric Allen

Smoke Blackbird had been away too long. The Lequires had seized the Blackbird farm, forcing the Indians and settlers off, and no one seemed willing to fight! He had to fight alone.

## THE THIRD RIDER
### Barry Cord

Mel Rawlins wasn't going to let anything stand in his way. His father was murdered, his two brothers gone. Now Mel rode for vengeance.

## BRETT RANDALL, GAMBLER
### E. B. Mann

Larry Day had the choice of running away from the law or of assuming a dead man's place. No matter what he decided he was bound to end up dead.

## THE GUNSHARP
### William R. Cox

The Eggerleys weren't very smart. They trained their sights on Will Carney and Arizona's biggest blood bath began.

## THE DEPUTY OF SAN RIANO
### Lawrence A. Keating and
### Al. P. Nelson

When a man fell dead from his horse, Ed Grant was spotted riding away from the scene. The deputy sheriff rode out after him and came up against everything from gunfire to dynamite.

## ARIZONA DRIFTERS
### W. C. Tuttle

When drifting Dutton and Lonnie Steelman decide to become partners they find that they have a common enemy in the formidable Thurston brothers.

## TOMBSTONE
### Matt Braun

Wells Fargo paid Luke Starbuck to outgun the silver-thieving stagecoach gang at Tombstone. Before long Luke can see the only thing bearing fruit in this eldorado will be the gallows tree.

## HIGH BORDER RIDERS
### Lee Floren

Buckshot McKee and Tortilla Joe cut the trail of a border tough who was running Mexican beef into Texas. They stopped the smuggler in his tracks.

# SUNDANCE: SILENT ENEMY
## John Benteen

A lone crazed Cheyenne was on a personal war path. They needed to pit one man against one crazed Indian. That man was Sundance.

# LASSITER
## Jack Slade

Lassiter wasn't the kind of man to listen to reason. Cross him once and he'll hold a grudge for years to come — if he let you live that long.

# LAST STAGE TO GOMORRAH
## Barry Cord

Jeff Carter, tough ex-riverboat gambler, now had himself a horse ranch that kept him free from gunfights and card games. Until Sturvesant of Wells Fargo showed up.

# HELL RIDERS
## Steve Mensing

Wade Walker's kid brother, Duane, was locked up in the Silver City jail facing a rope at dawn. Wade was a ruthless outlaw, but he was smart, and he had vowed to have his brother out of jail before morning!

# DESERT OF THE DAMNED
## Nelson Nye

The law was after him for the murder of a marshal — a murder he didn't commit. Breen was after him for revenge — and Breen wouldn't stop at anything . . . blackmail, a frameup . . . or murder.

# DAY OF THE COMANCHEROS
## Steven C. Lawrence

Their very name struck terror into men's hearts — the Comancheros, a savage army of cutthroats who swept across Texas, leaving behind a bloodstained trail of robbery and murder.